Robin Ray's ... ional debut was at the
age of four-a ... Reed's first
film, *Climbi* ...
worked exte ...
entertainm ...
his many c ...
radio as a ...
presenter ...
appearan ...
Music series.

An honours graduate of the Royal Academy of Dramatic Art, he returned there to become chief instructor in technique for four years, and he has also lectured on drama and literature for the British Council and the British Drama League.

He began producing plays as Associate Director of the Meadowbrook Theatre, Detroit, USA, and has since written and directed a theatrical anthology *Seven Deadly Sins* for the first Salisbury Festival, as well as composing the music for the West End revival of Anouilh's play *The Waltz of the Toreadors*.

Time For Lovers

A Personal Anthology

ROBIN RAY

SPHERE BOOKS LIMITED
30/32 Gray's Inn Road, London WC1X 8JL

First published in Great Britain by Weidenfeld & Nicolson Ltd 1975

Published by Sphere Books 1977

TRADE
MARK

Set in Monotype Plantin

Printed in Great Britain by
Hazell Watson & Viney Ltd
Aylesbury, Bucks

Contents

Acknowledgments

Works still in copyright are taken from the following sources, and reprinted by kind permission of the following publishers and individuals: 22 Mrs Nicolete Gray and the Society of Authors, on behalf of the Laurence Binyon Estate; 23 Frank Sidgwick, *More Verse*, Sidgwick and Jackson 1921; 23 John Betjeman, *Collected Poems*, John Murray; 24 Vladimir Nabokov, *Lolita*, Weidenfeld and Nicolson; 26 Hector Berlioz, *Memoirs*, translated David Cairns, Gollancz; 28 Roland Dalbiez Dessoir, *Psychoanalytical Method and the Doctrine of Freud*, translated T. F. Lindsay, Longmans; 29 Colette, *Claudine in Paris*, translated A. White, Secker and Warburg; 31 W. H. Auden, *Collected Shorter Poems*, Faber; 32 M. B. Yeats, Miss Anne Yeats, and Macmillan; 35 Heinrich Mann, *The Blue Angel*, Jarrolds; 42 Robert Graves, *Collected Poems 1965*, Cassell; 44 *For Love and Money*, The Bodley Head; 48 Dorothy Parker, *The Collected Dorothy Parker*, Duckworth; 50 Margot Asquith, *Autobiography*, Butterworth; 52 Paul Dehn, *Punch*; 52 Franklin P. Adams, *Such Stuff as Dreams*, in *So Much Velvet*, Doubleday; 56 The Estate of P. G. Wodehouse and Barrie and Jenkins; 62 Stephen Leacock, *The Bodley Head Stephen Leacock*, The Bodley Head; 65 C. S. Lewis, *The Screwtape Letters*, Collins; 66 Elinor Glyn, *Points of View*, Duckworth; 73 Margot Asquith, *Autobiography*, Butterworth; 78 Mrs Patrick Campbell, *My Life and Some Letters*, Hutchinson; 79 Robert Graves, *Collected Poems 1965*, Cassell; 81 Andrew Turnbull, *Scott Fitzgerald*, The Bodley Head; 83 Robert K. Massie, *Nicholas and Alexandra*, Gollancz; 90 Samuel Hoffenstein, *A Treasury of Humorous Verse*, Liveright; 93 Gustave Flaubert, *Madame Bovary*, translated Alan Russell, Penguin, Estate of Alan Russell; 94 Dorothy Parker, *The Collected Dorothy Parker*, Duckworth; 95 William Dickey, *Resolving Doubts*, *Saturday Review Magazine*; 97 Arthur Freeman, *Erotic Poetry*, Weidenfeld and Nicolson; 98 Erich Kästner, *The Moral Taxi Ride*, translated Jerome Dennis Rothenberg, *The Hudson Review*, X, 4; 99 Dorothy Parker, *The Collected Dorothy Parker*, Duckworth; 100 Arthur Rubinstein, *My Young Years*, Cape; 101 *La Rose d'Amour*, from *The Pearl*, New English Library; 102 Zoë Oldenbourg, *Catherine the Great*, translated Anne Carter, Heinemann; 103 Courtesy of the Estate of W. Somerset Maugham and Heinemann; 104 Stanley Kauffmann, *The Philanderer*, Secker and Warburg; 105 Terence Rattigan, *The Deep Blue Sea*, Hamish Hamilton and Rattigan Productions Ltd; 107 Graham Greene, *The End of the Affair*, courtesy of Graham Greene, Heinemann and The Bodley Head; 108 Jean Anouilh, *The Waltz of the Toreadors*, translated Lucienne Hill, French; 110 Jessica Mitford, *Hons and Rebels*, Gollancz; 112 Pierre La Mure, *Moulin Rouge*, Collins; 114 Michael Harrison, *Fanfare of Strumpets*, W. H. Allen; 117 John Press, *Guy Fawkes Night*, Oxford University Press; 118 Robert Payne, *Gershwin*, Robert Hale; 120 Sylvia Townsend Warner, *The Espalier*, Chatto and Windus; 123 Jean Anouilh, *Colombe*, translated Denis Cannan, Methuen; 124 George Gissing, *New Grub Street*, The Bodley Head; 127 Louis MacNiece, *Collected Poems*, Faber; 129 John Betjeman, *Collected Poems*, John Murray; 132 Philippa Pullar, *Consuming Passions*, Hamish Hamilton; 133 Stanley J. Sharpless, *In Praise of Cocoa*, *New Statesman*; 134 Earnest A. Hooton, from *What Cheer*, ed. David McCord, Coward McCann Inc.; 135 Irving Layton, *Erotic Poetry*, Weidenfeld and Nicolson; 138 Robert Graves, *I, Claudius*, Arthur Barker; 142 John Betjeman, *Collected Poems*, John Murray; 144 Jan Struther, *Freedom*, courtesy of Janet Graham and Oxford University Press; 145 Courtesy of M. B. Yeats, Miss Anne Yeats and Macmillan; 146 Nigel Nicolson, *Portrait of a Marriage*, Weidenfeld and Nicolson; 147 *Unnamed Sonnet*, courtesy of the Estate of the late Edna St Vincent Millay and Secker and Warburg; 147 Stephen Phillips, *The Apparition*, The Bodley Head; 148 Robert Graves, *Collected Poems 1965*, Cassell; 149 Ruth Feldman, *Sarcophagus Cover*, New York Times Co. and Macmillan NY.

Illustrations: frontispiece: *The Kiss*, Edvard Munch, 1895 (Albertina, Vienna); 20 Poster *Grafton Gallery of London*, Eugene Grasset, 1893 (Victoria and Albert Museum); 30 Oscar Wilde, detail from an engraving of spectators at the Parnell Commission, Royal Courts of Justice, February 1889 (Mansell Collection); 41 *The Lamplighter*, Joan Hassall, wood engraving illustrating *A Child's Garden of Verses* by Robert Louis Stevenson, Oxford University Press, 1946 (Weidenfeld and Nicolson Archive); 45 *The Single Bed*, Eric Gill, c.1930, illustration to *The Constant Mistress* (Victoria and Albert Museum); 49 *Dalliance*, Eric Gill, illustration to *Procreant Hymen*, Golden Cockerel Press, 1926 (Victoria and Albert Museum;) 60 Illustration by Henry Osporat to sonnet no. XCI 'Some glory in their birth . . .' from *Shakespeare's Sonnets*, The Bodley Head, 1899 (Weidenfeld and Nicolson Archive); 67 Illustration by Douglas Jerrold to *Mrs Candle's Curtain Lectures*, Charles Keene, 1866 (Victoria and Albert Museum); 81 *Falbales et Fanfreluches, Almanac des Modes*, G. Barbier, Paris, 1926 (Victoria and Albert Museum); 88 *Young Woman and Lust*, Urs Graf (Offentliche Kunstsammlung, Basle); 96 *The Hand under my Head*, Eric Gill, illustration to the *Song of Songs*, Golden Cockerel Press, 1925 (Victoria and Albert Museum); 115 Cora Pearl (Radio Times Hulton Picture Library); 122 D. H. Lawrence, by E. Kapp, 1923 (National Portrait Gallery, reproduced by courtesy of the artist); 130 Wood engraving by Joan Hassall, illustrating *All Day Long*, Oxford University Press, 1954 (Weidenfeld and Nicolson Archive); 150 Illustration to *Romantiques* by Paul Jarry (Radio Times Hulton Picture Library).

Picture research by Julia Brown.

The author and publisher have taken all possible care to trace the ownership of all works in copyright reprinted in this book, and to make acknowledgment for their use. If any errors have accidentally occurred, they will be corrected in subsequent editions, provided notification is sent to the publisher.

Preface

My first encounter with love was at the age of three, under the ping-pong table in the gamesroom of an hotel in Bournemouth. Actually, we were playing a game. It was called 'Doctors and Nurses', and my partner in medical passion was quite the most fascinating woman I had ever met. Unfortunately, my parents were keenly aware of the laws governing the practice of medicine without a licence, and so when they discovered our makeshift hospital, and learned the exact nature of the research in which we were engaged, the establishment was promptly closed.

Three years later, at a little school called 'The Hollies', I fell in love with Daphne. 'The Hollies' was really a girls' school, but boys were allowed there up to the age of about seven, to do sums and writing, and learn poetry and elocution and raffiawork. Mind you, Daphne wasn't in my class. She was two years older than I, so the only time I saw her was at the end of the day, when we waited in a line to be seen across the road by the teachers. Being in a higher class, Daphne was always in front. Most of the time I would spend admiring the back of her neck, and if ever, for some reason, she turned round, I would smile at her, raise my cap, and wish her good evening. At that, Daphne would turn to the front again, and then her friends would look round at me too, and shortly after that they would all giggle. I would keep smiling back, but, to tell the truth, I wasn't sure whether all the laughter was a good sign or a bad one.

There is an old saying: 'Scratch a good lover, and you will find a good son,' so I hope no one will accuse me of boasting when I tell you that I consulted my mother. My mother was in favour of a gift – come to think of it, my mother was always in favour of a gift – and so, one Saturday afternoon, we set off for Daphne's house, armed with a yellow, wooden pencil, with a fancy top made of sealing-wax, which sported a gay tassel. It had cost me my pocket money for that week, sevenpence. I think that Mamma had warned Daphne's mother that a suitor was on his way, but I certainly remember making the journey up the path to the front door alone, the pencil poised in my hand.

Of course, I knew exactly what was going to happen. She would open the door, I would raise my cap, say a few words of greeting and deliver my gift. It would please Daphne greatly, she would call her mother who would ask us both inside for tea and, while everyone talked, we would get to know each other and from then on walk home from school together every day.

Of course, it didn't happen like that at all but, all the same, it could have happened more nèatly than it did.

For a start, Daphne didn't open the door at all. That task was allocated to (perhaps even forced on?) her twelve-year-old sister, Barbara. Now Barbara was pretty, and I am sure Barbara was kind, but Barbara, however nice, was definitely not what I expected. I suppose I could have raised my cap and asked if Daphne was in. I could have waited until she came to the door, and then given her the yellow pencil with the fancy sealing-wax top and tassel. I could even have introduced her to my mother.

Alas, I did none of those things. I was so utterly amazed that the scene I had fixed in my mind had gone wrong from the very beginning, that it was as much as I could manage to launch into my prepared speech which, although not exactly Shakespeare, did have the virtue of extreme economy.

'I've brought you this pencil,' I said.

I must add that I did, at least, have the presence of mind to substitute 'Daphne' for 'you', and thus avoid total disaster. Barbara said that, if I would wait a moment, she would go inside and get her sister – but by then it was too late, I couldn't go through the effort of offering the wretched pencil yet again, and so I muttered something like 'It'll be all right if you take it', and started off at some speed down the path to my mother at the gate.

Before we both walked away, Daphne made a fleeting appearance in the doorway and waved. I took my cap off and smiled, and so things ended the way they had begun.

I have often wondered why I made no further efforts in Daphne's direction. I still used to see her every day at school, and at the end of each day she and her friends would still cross the road a few paces in front of me. I had visited her house, I had given her a pencil, surely I could have walked beside her for a bit, said a few words; it could have been so simple.

I think for all lovers there is a moment, an instant of time, when every relationship has to define its nature, when either a commitment must be made or everything must come to an end. Sometimes such a moment comes very early, sometimes late; but in my case, aged six, as I beat a foolish retreat down the garden path, my moment had found me wanting. My pride had proved more precious than my love, so that now Daphne has become an anecdote, rather than a memory.

I could not have known it at the time, but these two earliest episodes of my love-life were to dictate its entire pattern for the future. Modesty, gallantry and, above all, the laws of libel prevent me from entertaining you with later examples; through crushes on schoolteachers, crushes on fellow-pupils, my first 'French-kiss' (how wicked, how shattering), my first love affair, my first affair without love, but in each and every case it seems to me that I have been either presenting girls with yellow pencils with sealing-wax tops, or under the ping-pong table playing 'Doctors and Nurses'. Needless to say, those rare occasions when I was both holding the pencil and under the table have been by far the most important.

ROBIN RAY

Introduction

I have yet to read an anthology that did not include some kind of introduction, but I never fully understood why they were always necessary until I finished compiling this one. Try though one does to produce perfection there is always something to explain, something for which to apologize, and something that requires acknowledgment.

First, may I emphasize that this selection is a very personal one of my own favourite poems, essays, excerpts from novels, *bon mots* and the like, without any attempt to be comprehensive in a wider sense. It follows that some (the *Sonnet from the Portuguese* by Elizabeth Barrett Browning, or *Non Sum Qualis Eram* by Ernest Dowson) are likely to be well known, but unless the reader can recite such poems by heart I feel no shame in offering them once again. It also follows that I have made no attempt at impartiality; some authors, like John Betjeman and Robert Graves, appear frequently, others (dare I direct your attention to Shakespeare ?) not at all.

So much for what I have *not* tried to do – now for what I have. Unlike the more extensive anthology which a reader might use as a work of reference to dip into at random, it is my hope that *Time for Lovers* will be enjoyed as a book to be read from beginning to end, for that is the way I have conceived it. Although divided into four sections it is, in essence, a journey through love and thus life, from the joys and disillusions of Spring to the Summer of courtship and marriage, through Autumn's cynicism and compromise to Winter, and whatever, for each of us, that may hold. The contents of each section have been determined by the attitude of mind, rather than the actual age, of those who are writing or are depicted, and it is by this criterion, for example, that a letter from the forty-year-old Oscar Wilde to Lord Alfred Douglas is to be found under Spring.

Where commonsense has dictated that I make cuts or only use excerpts, I have done my best to make these selections as self-contained as possible, but I cherish the hope that they may whet the appetite of those not already familiar with them to turn to the entire work. If I had to mention two examples, pride of place would go to Anouilh's magnificent play *The Waltz of the Toreadors*, and the heart-stopping account of first love from Nabokov's *Lolita*, for me the greatest piece of prose in the entire collection.

I would also like to offer a special word of thanks to Antony Jay (*The Pick of the Rhubarb* – Hodder and Stoughton) and Kenneth Rose for the inspiration provided by their own excursions into the literature of love and to London University Library, the Westminster Public Library, and Bernard Levin for their generous assistance with dates I was unable to trace.

Finally, it is one thing vaguely to recall a poem or a piece of literature that has given you pleasure, but during the preparation of this book I have found that it is quite another to identify correctly, and hunt out, each and every one. To be quite honest I doubt whether I could have done so, and so gladly take this opportunity to express my gratitude to, and admiration for, Sybil Welch, who did.

R.R.

Spring

First love is a kind of vaccination which saves a man from catching the complaint a second time.

HONORÉ DE BALZAC (1799–1850)

O World, be nobler, for her sake!
  If she but knew thee what thou art,
What wrongs are borne, what deeds are done
In thee beneath thy daily sun,
  Know'st thou not that her tender heart
For pain and very shame would break?
O World, be nobler, for her sake!

LAURENCE BINYON (1869–1943)
O World, Be Nobler

Love should run out to meet love with open arms. Indeed, the ideal story is that of two people who go into love step for step, with a fluttered consciousness, like a pair of children venturing together into a dark room. From the first moment when they see each other, with a pang of curiosity, through stage after stage of growing pleasure and embarrassment, they can read the expression of their own trouble in each other's eyes. There is here no declaration properly so called; the feeling is so plainly shared, that as soon as the man knows what it is in his own heart, he is sure of what is in the woman's.

This simple accident of falling in love is as beneficial as it is astonishing.

ROBERT LOUIS STEVENSON (1850–1894)
Virginibus Puerisque

[*A sonnet is a poem fourteen lines long, in rhyming couplets, containing a question and an answer. This must be the shortest ever written, a brilliant little* tour de force *by Frank Sidgwick entitled 'The Aeronaut to his Lady'.*]

I
Through
Blue
Sky
Fly
To
You
Why?
Sweet
Love
Feet
Move
So
Slow.

Oh but Wendy, when the carpet yielded to my indoor
  pumps
 There you stood, your gold hair streaming,
 Handsome in the hall-light gleaming
There you looked and there you led me off into the game
  of clumps
 Then the new Victrola playing
 And your funny uncle saying
Choose your partners for a fox-trot! Dance until its *tea*
  o'clock!
 'Come on, young'uns, foot it featly!'
 Was it chance that paired us neatly,
 I, who loved you so completely,
You, who pressed me closely to you, hard against your
  party frock?

'Meet me when you've finished eating!' So we met and
no one found us.
Oh that dark and furry cupboard while the rest played
hide and seek!
Holding hands our two hearts beating in the bedroom
silence round us,
Holding hands and hardly hearing sudden footsteps,
thud and shriek.
Love that lay too deep for kissing –
'Where *is* Wendy? Wendy's missing!'
Love so pure it *had* to end,
Love so strong that I was frighten'd
When you gripped my fingers tight and
Hugging, whispered 'I'm your friend'.

JOHN BETJEMAN (born 1906)
From *Indoor Games at Newbury*

All at once we were madly, clumsily, shamelessly, agonizingly in love with each other; hopelessly, I should add, because that frenzy of mutual possession might have been assuaged only by our actually imbibing and assimilating every particle of each other's soul and flesh; but there we were, unable even to mate as slum children would have so easily found an opportunity to do. After one wild attempt we made to meet at night in her garden (of which more later), the only privacy we were allowed was to be out of earshot but not out of sight of the populous part of the 'plage'. There, on the soft sand, a few feet away from our elders, we would sprawl all morning, in a petrified paroxysm of desire, and take advantage of every blessed quirk in space and time to touch each other: her hand, half-hidden in the sand, would creep toward me, its slender brown fingers sleepwalking nearer and nearer, then her opalescent knee would start on a long cautious journey; sometimes a chance rampart built by younger children granted us sufficient concealment to graze each other's salty lips; these incomplete contacts drove our healthy and inexperienced young bodies to such a state of exasperation that not even the cool blue water, under which we still clawed at each other, could bring relief.

Among some treasure I lost during the wanderings of my adult years, there was a snapshot taken by my aunt which showed Annabel, her parents and the staid, elderly lame gentleman, a Dr Cooper, who that same summer courted my aunt, grouped around a table in a sidewalk café. Annabel did not come out well, caught as she was in the act of bending over her 'chocolat glacé', and her thin bare shoulders and the parting in her hair were about all that could be identified (as I remember that picture) amid the sunny blur into which her lost loveliness graded; but I, sitting somewhat apart from the rest, came out with a kind of dramatic conspicuousness: a moody, beetle-browed boy in a dark sport shirt and well-tailored white shorts, his legs crossed, sitting in profile, looking away. That photograph was taken on the last day of our fatal summer and just a few minutes before we made our second and final attempt to thwart fate. Under the flimsiest of pretexts (this was our very last chance, and nothing really mattered) we escaped from the café to the beach, and found a desolate stretch of sand, and there, in the violet shadow of some red rocks forming a kind of cave, had a brief session of avid caresses, with somebody's lost pair of sunglasses for only witness. I was on my knees, and on the point of possessing my darling, when two bearded bathers, the old man of the sea and his brother, came out of the sea with exclamations of ribald encouragement, and four months later she died of typhus in Corfu.

VLADIMIR NABOKOV (born 1899)
Lolita

Will it be credited that when I was only twelve years old, and even before I fell under the spell of music, I became the victim of that cruel passion so well described by the Mantuan?

My mother's father, who bore a name immortalised by Scott–Marmion – lived at Meylan, about seven miles from Grenoble. This district, with its scattered hamlets, the valley of the winding Isère, the Dauphiny mountains that here join a spur of the Alps, is one of the most romantic spots I know. Here my mother, my sisters, and I usually passed three weeks towards the end of summer.

Now and then my uncle, Felix Marmion, who followed the fiery track of the great Emperor, would pay a flying visit during our stay, wreathed with cannon smoke and ornamented with a fine sabre cut across the face. He was then only adjutant-major in the Lancers; but the young gallant, ready to lay down his life for one look from his leader, he believed the throne of Napoleon as stable as Mont Blanc. His taste for music made him a great addition to our gay little circle, for he both sang and played the violin well.

High over Meylan, nicked in a crevice of the mountain, stands a little white house, half-hidden amidst its vineyards and gardens, behind which rise the woods, the barren hills, a ruined tower, and St Eynard – a frowning mass of rock.

This sweet secluded spot, evidently predestined to romance, was the home of Madame Gautier, who lived there with two nieces, of whom the younger was called Estelle. Her name at once caught my attention from its being that of the heroine of Florian's pastoral *Estelle and Némorin*, which I had filched from my father's library, and read a dozen times in secret.

Estelle was just eighteen – tall, graceful, with large, grave, questioning eyes that yet could smile, hair worthy to ornament the helmet of Achilles, and feet – I will not say Andalusian, but pure Parisian, and on those little feet she wore . . . pink slippers!

Never before had I seen pink slippers. Do not smile; I have forgotten the colour of her hair (I fancy it was black), yet, never do I recall Estelle but, in company with the flash of her large eyes, comes the twinkle of her dainty pink shoes. I had been struck by lightning. To say I loved her comprises everything. I hoped for, expected, knew nothing but that I was wretched, dumb, despairing. By night I suffered agonies, by day I wandered alone through the fields of Indian corn, or sought, like a wounded bird, the deepest recesses of my grandfather's orchard.

Jealousy – dread comrade of love – seized me at the least word spoken by a man to my divinity; even now I shudder at the clank of a spur, remembering the noise of my uncle's while dancing with her.

Everyone in the neighbourhood laughed at the piteously precocious child torn by his obsession. Perhaps Estelle laughed too, for she soon guessed all.

One evening, I remember, there was a party at Madame Gautier's, and we played prisoner's base. The men were bidden choose their partners, and I was purposely told to choose first. But I dared not, my heart-beats choked me; I lowered my eyes unable to speak. They were beginning to tease me when Estelle, smiling down from her beauteous height, caught my hand, saying: 'Come! I will begin; I choose Monsieur Hector.' But ah! she laughed!

Does time heal all wounds; do other loves efface the first? Alas, no! With me time is powerless. Nothing wipes out the memory of my first love.

I was thirteen when we parted. I was thirty when, returning from Italy, I passed near St Eynard again. My eyes filled with tears at the sight of the little white house – the ruined tower. I loved her still!

On reaching home I heard that she was married; but even that could not cure me. A few days later my mother said: 'Hector, will you take this letter to the coach-office. It is for a lady who will be in the Vienne diligence. While they change horses ask the guard for Madame F., give her this letter, and look carefully at her. You may recognize her, although you have not met for seventeen years.'

Without suspicion I went on my errand and asked for

Madame F. 'I am she, Monsieur', said a voice that thrilled my heart. 'It is Estelle', said my heart. Estelle! still lovely, still the nymph, the hamadryad of Meylan's green slopes. Still lovely with her proud carriage, her glorious hair, her dazzling smile. But ah! where were the little pink shoes?

She took the letter. Did she know me? I could not tell, but I returned home quite upset by the meeting. My mother smiled at me. 'So Némorin has not forgotten his Estelle', she said. *His* Estelle! Mother! mother! was that trick quite fair?

HECTOR BERLIOZ (1803–1869)
Memoirs
(translated by David Cairns)

Love, like the measles, attacks only the young.

Later childhood is the stage of undifferentiated sexual inclination, when there appears an object, often also an aim, towards which love tends. But as yet there exists no differentiation such as that the object must purely and simply belong to the opposite sex. Often such inclinations are rather directed towards persons of the same sex, animals – in short, any living creature – and this stage may continue as far as the twentieth year, but may often begin at the fourth or fifth. Similarly, during these years the aim is not as yet predetermined. . . . Perverse contacts, embraces, or acts are a very frequent aim during these years, whether their object belongs to the same or to the opposite sex.

ROLAND DALBIEZ DESSOIR
Psychoanalytical Method and the Doctrine of Freud

[*A letter from Charlie to his boy-friend Marcel. Both are adolescent schoolboys.*]

My Darling,

I am going to look up that story . . . and I shall translate for you the passages that describe the passionate friendship of the two children. I know German as well as I know French, so this translation won't give me the least difficulty. I almost regret this because it would have been a delight to me to endure some hardships for you, my only loved one.

Oh, yes, my only one! My only loved, my only adored one! And to think your jealousy, always on the alert, is flaring up again! Don't say it isn't, I know how to read between your lines as I know how to read the depths of your eyes and I cannot misunderstand the irritable little sentence in your letter about 'the new friend with the too-black curls whose conversation absorbed me so much at the four o'clock break'.

This so-called new friend – actually I hardly know him – this little boy 'with the too-black curls' (why *too* ?) is a Florentine . . . whom his parents have sent as a boarder to B——, the celebrated philosophy beak, to remove him from the depravity of school friendships; he's certainly got far-seeing parents. . . !

My slender, my adorable child, my supple, living Tanagra, I kiss your throbbing eyes. You know very well that all that unwholesome past I sacrified without hesitation for you, all that past with its degrading curiosities that now I loathe, seems to me today like some distant, horrible nightmare. Only your tenderness remains, inspiring me, firing me. . . .

Yours, body and soul,
Your Charlie

COLETTE (1873–1954)
Claudine in Paris
(translated by A. White)

Dearest of all Boys,

Your letter was delightful, red and yellow wine to me; but I am sad and out of sorts. Bosie, you must not make scenes with me. They kill me, they wreck the loveliness of life. I cannot see you, so Greek and gracious, distorted with passion. I cannot listen to your curved lips saying hideous things to me. I would sooner . . . be blackmailed by every renter in London . . . than have you bitter, unjust, hating. I must see you soon. You are the divine thing I want, the thing of grace and beauty; but I don't know how to do it. Shall I come to Salisbury? My bill here is £49 for a week. I have also got a new sitting-room over the Thames. Why are you not here, my dear, my wonderful boy? I fear I must leave; no money, no credit, and a heart of lead.

Your Own Oscar

OSCAR WILDE (1854–1900)
Letters
Letter to Lord Alfred Douglas, March 1893

Oh the valley in the summer where I and my John
Beside the deep river would walk on and on
While the flowers at our feet and the birds up above
Argued so sweetly on reciprocal love,
And I leaned on his shoulder; 'O Johnny, let's play':
But he frowned like thunder and he went away.

O that Friday near Christmas as I well recall
When we went to the Charity Matinée Ball,
The floor was so smooth and the band was so loud
And Johnny so handsome I felt so proud;
'Squeeze me tighter, dear Johnny, let's dance till it's day':
But he frowned like thunder and he went away.

Shall I ever forget at the Grand Opera
When music poured out of each wonderful star?
Diamonds and pearls they hung dazzling down
Over each silver or golden silk gown;
'O John I'm in Heaven', I whispered to say:
But he frowned like thunder and he went away.

O but he was fair as a garden in flower,
As slender and tall as the great Eiffel Tower
When the waltz throbbed out on the long promenade
O his eyes and his smile they went straight to my heart;
'O marry me, Johnny, I'll love and obey':
But he frowned like thunder and he went away.

O last night I dreamed of you, Johnny, my lover,
You'd the sun on one arm and the moon on the other,
The sea it was blue and the grass it was green,
Every star rattled a round tambourine;
Ten thousand miles deep in a pit where I lay:
But you frowned like thunder and you went away.

W. H. AUDEN (1907–1973)
Johnny (from *Four Cabaret Songs*)

His body was as straight as Circe's wand:
Jove might have sipt out nectar from his hand.
Even as delicious meat is to the tast,
So was his neck in touching, and surpast
The white of Pelops' shoulder: I could tell ye
How smooth his breast was, and how white his belly,
And whose immortal fingers did imprint
That heavenly path with many a curious dint,
That runs along his back; but my rude pen
Can hardly blazon forth the loves of men,
Much less of powerful gods: let it suffice
That my slack Muse sings of Leander's eyes;
Those orient cheeks and lips, exceeding his
That leapt into the water for a kiss
Of his own shadow, and, despising many,
Died ere he could enjoy the love of any.

CHRISTOPHER MARLOWE (1564–1593)
Hero and Leander

Down by the salley gardens my love and I did meet;
She pass'd the salley gardens with little snow-white feet.
She bid me take love easy, as the leaves grow on the tree;
But I, being young and foolish, with her would not agree.

In a field by the river my love and I did stand,
And on my leaning shoulder she laid her snow-white hand.
She bid me take life easy, as the grass grows on the weirs;
But I was young and foolish, and now am full of tears.

W. B. YEATS (1865–1939)
Down by the Salley Gardens

Breathless, we flung us on the windy hill,
Laughed in the sun, and kissed the lovely grass.
You said, 'Through glory and ecstacy we pass;
Wind, sun, and earth remain, the birds sing still,
When we are old, are old. . . .' 'And when we die
All's over that is ours; and life burns on
Through other lovers, other lips', said I,
'Heart of my heart, our heaven is now, is won!'

'We are Earth's best, that learnt her lesson here.
Life is our cry. We have kept the faith!' we said;
'We shall go down with unreluctant tread
Rose-crowned into the darkness! 'Proud we were
And laughed, that had such brave true things to say.
– And then you suddenly cried, and turned away.

RUPERT BROOKE (1887–1915)
The Hill

Never seek to tell thy love,
  Love that never told can be;
For the gentle wind doth move
  Silently, invisibly.

I told my love, I told my love,
  I told her all my heart,
Trembling, cold, in ghastly fears.
  Ah! She did depart!

Soon after she was gone from me,
  A traveller came by,
Silently, invisibly:
  He took her with a sigh.

WILLIAM BLAKE (1757–1827)
Love's Secret

A man should never tear his hair
When jilted by his lady fair,
She isn't apt to be enthralled
The least bit more if he is bald.

RICHARD WHEELER (born 1922)

I tore the locket which contained her hair (and which I used to wear continually in my bosom as the precious token of her dear regard) from my neck and trampled it in pieces. I could not stay in the room – I could not leave it – my rage, my despair were uncontrollable. I shrieked curses on her name and on her false love and the scream I uttered (so pitiful and piercing was it that the sound of it terrified me) instantly brought the whole house: father, mother, lodgers and all, into the room. They thought I was destroying her and myself. . . . I gathered up the fragments of the locket of her hair which were strewed about the floor, kissed them, folded them up in a sheet of paper and sent them to her with these lines written in pencil on the outside: 'Pieces of a broken heart, to be kept in remembrance of the unhappy. Farewell.' I was stung with scorpions – my flesh crawled; I was choked with rage. She started up in her own likeness, a serpent in place of a woman. She had fascinated, she had stung me and had returned to her proper shape, gliding from me after inflicting the mortal wound and instilling deadly poison into every pore; but her form lost none of its original brightness by the change of character but was all glittering, beauteous, voluptuous grace. Seed of the serpent or of the woman, she was divine! I was transformed too, no longer human. . . . And yet, in some sense I am proud that I can feel this dreadful passion – it gives me a kind of rank in the kingdom of love.

WILLIAM HAZLITT (1778–1830)
Liber Amoris

He had left the courtroom during that burst of laughter, hastening as if dams had broken, clouds burst and volcanoes erupted. His world had come tumbling about his ears – for she was a harlot! . . . She had no decency; anyone could share her! . . . And he was utterly surprised. That she should prove untrustworthy! Until today – until this terrible moment – she had seemed his other self; and now she had torn herself from his heart. He could see that inner wound bleeding, and could not understand it. Since he had had no intimate relations with others he had never been deceived before, and now he suffered like a child. . . . He suffered uncouthly, with bewilderment.

He went home. At the first word his servant spoke, he broke into a rage and chased her out of the house. Then he flew into his room, locked the door, threw himself onto the sofa and groaned. Utterly ashamed, he pulled himself together and took out his MS on the particles of Homer. . . . But sheet after sheet had drafts of letters to Rosa – others notes of some favourable criticism concerning her. There was no more paper; he had thoughtlessly spoilt it all. He saw even his work undermined by her, his thoughts absorbed by her, his whole life come to an end through her. . . .

Night had fallen and from the darkness her bright whimsical, teasing face looked out at him; he turned his eyes from it with anguish. For he felt it the index to every shame. She belonged to – everyone. He hid his face in his hand – the blood had rushed to his cheeks. This late-blooming sensuality – moving like a slow corruption through his dried-up body, changing the whole current of his life and driving him to hysterical extremes – was now torturing him with remembered pictures. He saw her in her little room at the *Blue Angel* – watched her alluring hands – those hands that had first beckoned him to love. That teasing glance – provocative. But glance and hands were beckoning now to another. . . . He watched the whole thing happen – he saw her dancing – and he sobbed – he sobbed!

HEINRICH MANN (1871–1950)
The Blue Angel

To be in love is merely to be in a state of perpetual anaesthesia – to mistake an ordinary young man for a Greek god or an ordinary young woman for a goddess.

H. L. Mencken (1880–1956)

Werther had a love for Charlotte
  Such as words could never utter;
Would you know how first he met her?
  She was cutting bread and butter.

Charlotte was a married lady,
  And a moral man was Werther,
And, for all the wealth of Indies,
  Would do nothing for to hurt her.

So he sighed and pined and ogled,
  And his passion boiled and bubbled,
Till he blew his silly brains out,
  And no more was by it troubled.

Charlotte, having seen his body
  Borne before her on a shutter,
Like a well-conducted person
  Went on cutting bread and butter.

William Makepeace Thackeray (1811–1863)
Sorrows of Werther

[*Extracts from Letters written by Charlotte Brontë to M. Heger, her professor in Brussels, for whom she had developed a passion which was not returned.*]

Day and night I find neither rest nor peace. If I sleep I am disturbed by tormenting dreams in which I see you, always severe, always grave, always incensed against me. Forgive me then, Monsieur, if I adopt the course of writing to you again. How can I endure life if I make no effort to ease its sufferings ? . . .

Monsieur, the poor have not need of much to sustain them – they ask only for the crumbs that fall from the rich men's table. But if they are refused they die of hunger. Nor do I either, need much affection from those I love. . . . But you showed me of yore a *little* interest, when I was your pupil in Brussels, and I hold on to the maintenance of that *little* interest – I hold on to it as I would hold on to life.

[Nearly a year later] I tell you frankly that I have tried meanwhile to forget you. . . . I have done everything; I have sought occupations; I have denied myself absolutely the pleasure of speaking about you – even to Emily; but I have been able to conquer neither my regrets nor my impatience. . . . To write to an old pupil cannot be a very interesting occupation for you, I know; but for me it is life. Your last letter was stay and prop to me – nourishment to me for half a year. . . . To forbid me to write to you, to refuse to answer me, would be to tear from me my only joy on earth, to deprive me of my last privilege. . . . When day by day I await a letter, and when day by day disappointment comes to fling me back into overwhelming sorrow, and the sweet delight of seeing your handwriting and reading your counsel escapes me . . . then fever claims me – I lose appetite and sleep – I pine away.

CHARLOTTE BRONTË (1816–1855)
Letters

[*Another master-pupil relationship Abelard, the great scholar, had been engaged (by her uncle) to instruct Heloïse. When the scandal of their great love affair broke, her uncle had Abelard castrated. Heloïse retired to a nunnery, but still wrote passionate letters to her former lover.*]

It is difficult to snatch one's soul away from its greatest love – and the pleasures of the love we knew together are so sweet to me that the memory of them can *never in any way* be effaced from my memory. They are with me always, they accompany me wherever I go, they do not even spare my sleep . . . and there are times even when I pray that the images and pleasurable scenes of our love-making stir my miserable heart until the voluptuous memories of those moments even distract me from my prayers – and people praise my chastity – when in reality I am aflame with desire to again relive those passions we have together experienced. I beg of you, Abelard . . . to remember always that it was for you alone, and not for divine vocation, that I donned my monastic habit.

HELOÏSE (?1098–1164)
Letter to Abelard (1079– ?1144)
(translated by Leonard Melling)

This was a journey of adventures and knight-errantry. One of the lady's servants being . . . desperately in love with Mrs Howard's woman . . . the amorous and jealous youth having a little drink in his pate, had here killed himself had he not been prevented; for, alighting from his horse, and drawing his sword, he endeavoured twice or thrice to fall on it, but was interrupted by our coachman, and a stranger passing by. After this, running to his rival, and snatching his sword from his side (for we had beaten his own out of his hand), and on the sudden pulling down his mistress, would have run both of them through; we parted them, not without some blood. This miserable creature poisoned himself for her not many days after they came to London.

JOHN EVELYN (1620–1706)
Diary
15 July 1675

I walked with Maisie long years back
  The streets of Camden Town,
I splendid in my suit of black,
  And she divine in brown.

Hers was a proud and noble face,
  A secret heart, and eyes
Like water in a lonely place
  Beneath unclouded skies.

A bed, a chest, a faded mat,
  And broken chairs a few,
Were all we had to grace our flat
  In Hazel Avenue.

But I could walk to Hampstead Heath,
  And crown her head with daisies,
And watch the streaming world beneath,
  And men with other Maisies.

When I was ill and she was pale
  And empty stood our store,
She left the latchkey on its nail,
  And saw me nevermore.

Perhaps she cast herself away
  Lest both of us should drown.
Perhaps she feared to die, as they
  Who die in Camden Town.

What came of her ? The bitter nights
  Destroy the rose and lily,
And souls are lost among the lights
  Of painted Piccadilly.

What came of her ? The river flows
  So deep and wide and stilly,
And waits to catch the fallen rose
  And clasp the broken lily.

I dream she dwells in London still
    And breathes the evening air,
And often walk to Primrose Hill,
    And hope to meet her there.

Once more together we will live,
    For I will find her yet:
I have so little to forgive;
    So much I can't forget.

JAMES ELROY FLECKER (1884–1915)
The Ballad of Camden Town

His eyes are quickened so with grief,
He can watch a grass or leaf
Every instant grow; he can
Clearly through a flint wall see,
Or watch the startled spirit flee
From the throat of a dead man.

Across two counties he can hear
And catch your words before you speak.
The woodlouse or the maggot's weak
Clamour rings in his sad ear,
And noise so slight it would surpass
Credence – drinking sound of grass,
Worm talk, clashing jaws of moth
Chumbling holes in cloth;
The groan of ants who undertake
Gigantic loads for honour's sake
(Their sinews creak, their breath comes thin);
Whir of spiders when they spin,
And minute whispering, mumbling, sighs
Of idle grubs and flies.

This man is quickened so with grief,
He wanders god-like or like thief,
Inside and out, below, above,
Without relief seeking lost love.

ROBERT GRAVES (born 1895)
Lost Love

He who tries to forget a woman has never loved her.

. . . This unfortunate youth, whose name was Smith, and who was a shoemaker, was in love with a young woman, who, in spite of all his importunities and his proofs of ardent passion, refused to marry him, and even discovered her liking for another; and he, unable to support life, accompanied by the thought of her being in possession of anybody but himself, put an end to his life by the means of a rope. . . .

Poor Smith, who was at this age of love and madness, might surely be presumed to have done the deed in a moment of 'temporary mental derangement'. He was an object of compassion in every humane breast: he had parents . . . and kindred and friends to lament his death, and to feel shame at the disgrace inflicted on his lifeless body: *yet* he was pronounced to be a 'felo de se' or self-murderer, and his body was put into a hole by the wayside, with a stake driven through it.

WILLIAM COBBETT (1762–1835)
Advice to Young Men

[Roger Wright and Emma Railton died on 15th March 1715; having . . .] dyed for love, his parents would not lett him marry the one he loved and who loved him so well that when the passing bell went for him, she fell down and swooned away and lived but till next morning – her heart broke at hearing it. They were buryed together.

Epitaph on a tablet in the west wall of Bowes church

Coffee-cups cool on the Vicar's harmonium
  Clock fingers creep to a quarter to ten.
Softly, like patter of mouse-feet, the whisper
  Of busy lead pencil and ball-pointed pen.

Separate hands scribble separate phrases –
  Innocent, each, as the new-driven snow.
What will they spell when the paper's unfolded?
  Lucifer, only, and Belial know.

'Ready, Miss Montague? Come, Mr Jellaby!'
  (Peek at your papers and finger your chins)
'Shy, Mr Pomfret? You'd rather the Vicar . . . ?
  Oh, good for the Vicar'. The Vicar begins:

'FAT MR POMFRET met FROWSTY MISS MONTAGUE
  UNDER THE BACK SEAT IN JELLABY'S CART.
He said to her: "WILL YOU DO WHAT I WANT YOU TO?"
  She said to him: "THERE'S A SONG IN MY HEART!".'

What was the consequence? What did the World say?
  List, in the silence, to Damocles' sword!
Today Mr Pomfret has left for Karachi
  And little Miss Montague screams in her ward.

PAUL DEHN (born 1912)
A Game of Consequences

Of all sexual aberrations, perhaps the most peculiar is chastity.

RÉMY DE GOURMONT (1858–1915)

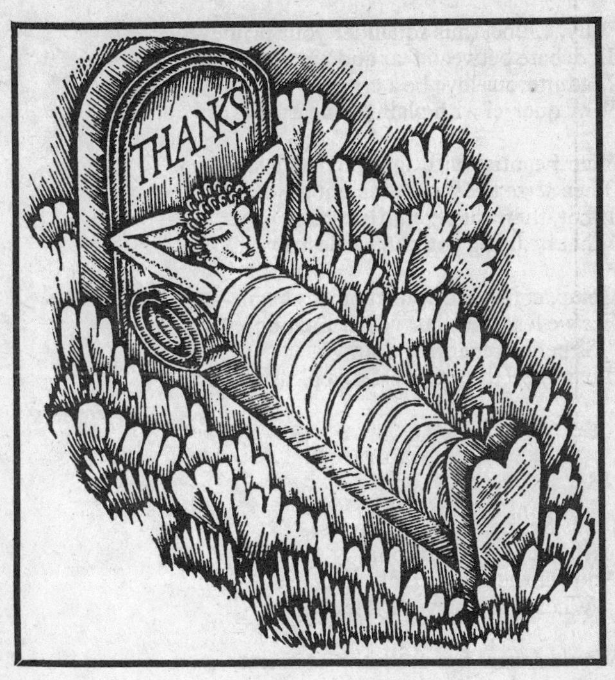

No, no, for my Virginity,
When I lose that, says Rose, I'll dye;
Behind the elmes last night, cry'd Dick,
Rose, were you not extremely sick?

MATTHEW PRIOR (1664–1721)
A True Maid

Why, Chloë, thus squander your prime
In debate between fear and temptation?
If adulterous love be a crime,
Why quarrel with plain fornication?

Your beauties with age you may lose;
Then seize the short moment of joy.
If not, then with confidence use
What by using you cannot destroy.

Come, come, bid your raptures begin
Ere we lose both our youth and our leisure.
'Tis better repenting a sin
Than regretting the loss of a pleasure.

Pious Selinda goes to prayers,
  If I but ask the favour;
And yet the tender fool's in tears,
  When she believes I'll leave her.

Would I were free from this restraint,
  Or else had hopes to win her:
Would she could make of me a saint,
  Or I of her a sinner.

William Congreve (1670–1729)
Pious Selinda

I am ready to die, sweetheart, if it be thy will; allay his thirst who thy star hath scorched and undone; the fountains and rivers deny no man drink that comes; the fountain doth not say, Thou shall not drink; nor the apple, Thou shall not eat; nor the fair meadow, Walk not in me; but thou alone wilt not let me come near thee or see thee; condemned and despised, I die for grief.

ROBERT BURTON (1577–1640
Anatomy of Melancholy
Philostratus, in an epistle to his mistress

Go, lovely Rose!
Tell her, that wastes her time and me,
That now she knows,
When I resemble her to thee,
How sweet and fair she seems to be.

Tell her that's young,
And shuns to have her graces spied,
That hadst thou sprung
In deserts where no men abide,
Thou must have uncommended died.

Small is the worth
Of beauty from the light retired:
Bid her come forth,
Suffer herself to be desired,
And not blush so to be admired.

Then die – that she
The common fate of all things rare
May read in thee;
How small a part of time they share
That are so wondrous sweet and fair?

EDMUND WALLER (1606–1687)
Go, Lovely Rose!

A single flow'r he sent me, since we met.
All tenderly his messenger he chose;
Deep-hearted, pure, with scented dew still wet –
One perfect rose.

I knew the language of the floweret;
'My fragile leaves', it said, 'his heart enclose'.
Love long has taken for his amulet
One perfect rose.

Why is it no one ever sent me yet
One perfect limousine, do you suppose?
Ah no, it's always just my luck to get
One perfect rose.

DOROTHY PARKER (1893–1967)
One Perfect Rose

The red rose whispers of passion,
And the white rose breathes of love;
O, the red rose is a falcon,
And the white rose is a dove.

But I send you a cream-white rosebud
With a flush on its petal tips;
For the love that is purest and sweetest
Has a kiss of desire on the lips.

JOHN BOYLE O'REILLY (1844–1890)
A White Rose

Kiss, if you can. Resistance if she make,
And will not give you Kisses, let her take.
'Fie, fie, you naughty man' are Words of Course;
She struggles, but to be subdu'd by Force.
Kiss only soft, I charge you, and beware,
With your hard bristles not to brush the Fair.
He who has gain'd a Kiss, and gains no more,
Deserves to lose the Bliss he got before.
If once she kiss, her Meaning is exprest;
There wants but little Pushing for the rest.

OVID (43 BC–AD 18 ?)
Arts of Love
(translated from the Latin by John Dryden (1631–1700))

When the lips of two lovers are brought into direct contact with each other, it is called a 'straight kiss'.

When the heads of two lovers are bent towards each other, and when so bent, kissing takes place, it is called 'a bent kiss'.

When one of them turns up the face of the other by holding the head and chin, and then kissing, it is called a 'turned kiss'.

When the lower lip is pressed with much force, it is called a 'pressed kiss'.

The Kama Sutra of Vatsayana

Some say kissing is a sin, but if it was na lawful, lawyers would na allow it; if it was na holy, ministers would na do it; if it was na modest, maidens would na take it; if it was na plenty, puir folk would na get it!

ROBERT BURNS (1759–1796)

On the second night of his visit, our distinguished guest [Sir Charles Dilke] met Laura in the passage on her way to bed; he said to her: 'If you will kiss me, I will give you a signed photograph of myself.' To which she answered: 'It is awfully good of you, Sir Charles, but I would rather not, for what on earth should I do with the photograph?'

MARGOT ASQUITH (1864–1945)
Autobiography

They say there's microbes in a kiss,
This rumor is most rife,
Come, lady dear, and make of me
An invalid for life.

The fountains mingle with the river
  And the rivers with the Ocean,
The Winds of Heaven mix for ever
  With a sweet emotion;
Nothing in the world is single;
  All things by a law divine
In one spirit meet and mingle.
  Why not I with thine?

See the mountains kiss high Heaven
  And the waves clasp one another;
No sister-flower would be forgiven
  If it disdained its brother;
And the sunlight clasps the earth
  And the moonbeams kiss the sea:
What is all this sweet work worth
  If thou kiss not me?

PERCY BYSSHE SHELLEY (1792–1822)
Love's Philosophy

Jenny kiss'd me when we met,
  Jumping from the chair she sat in;
Time, you thief, who love to get
  Sweets into your list, put that in!
Say I'm weary, say I'm sad,
  Say that health and wealth have missed me,
Say I'm growing old, but add,
  Jenny kiss'd me.

LEIGH HUNT (1784–1859)
Jenny Kiss'd Me

Jenny kiss'd me when we met,
  Jumping from the chair she sat in;
Time, you thief, who love to get
  Sweets into your lists, put that in!
Say I'm weary, say I'm old,
  Say that health and wealth have missed me,
Say I've had a filthy cold
  Since Jenny kiss'd me.

PAUL DEHN (born 1912)

Jenny kiss'd me in a dream;
  So did Elsie, Lucy, Cora,
Bessie, Gwendolyn, Eupheme,
  Alice, Adelaide and Dora.
Say of honor I'm devoid,
  Say monogamy has miss'd me,
But don't say to Dr Freud
  Jenny kiss'd me.

FRANKLIN P. ADAMS (1881–1960)

Calf love – following a girl on a windy day.

Whether he had forgotten what it felt like, or his head had really grown bigger since the summer before, Henry could not decide. But his straw hat hurt him: it pinched his forehead and started a dull ache in the two bones just over the temples. So he chose a corner seat in a third class 'smoker', took off his hat and put it in the rack with his large black cardboard portfolio and his Aunt B's Christmas-present gloves. The carriage smelt horribly of wet india-rubber and soot. There were ten minutes to spare before the train went, so Henry decided to go and have a look at the book-stall....

He found an anthology of English poetry, and went on turning the pages, until he became conscious of shouting and shuffling, and he looked up to see the train moving slowly.

'God's thunder!' Henry dashed forward. A man with a flag and a whistle had his hand on a door. He clutched Henry somehow.... Henry was inside with the door slammed, in a carriage that wasn't a 'smoker', that had not a trace of his straw hat or the black portfolio or his Aunt B's Christmas-present gloves. Instead, in the opposite corner, close against the wall, there sat a girl. Henry did not dare to look at her, but he felt certain she was staring at him. 'She must think I'm mad', he thought, 'dashing into a train without even a hat, and in the evening, too.' He felt so funny. He didn't know how to sit or sprawl. He put his hands in his pockets and tried to appear quite indifferent and frown at a large photograph of Bolton Abbey. But feeling her eyes on him he gave her just the tiniest glance. Quickly she looked away out of the window, and then Henry, careful of her slightest movement, went on looking. She sat pressed against the window, her cheek and shoulder half hidden by a long wave of marigold-coloured hair. One little hand in a grey cotton glove held a leather case on her lap with the initials E.M. on it. The other hand she had slipped through the window-strap, and Henry noticed a silver bangle on the wrist with a Swiss cow-bell and a silver shoe and a fish. She wore a green coat and a hat with a wreath round it....

That moment the girl turned around and, catching his glance, she blushed. She bent her head to hide the red colour that flew in her cheeks, and Henry, terribly embarrassed, blushed too. 'I shall have to speak – have to – have to!' He started putting up his hand to raise the hat that wasn't there. He thought that funny; it gave him confidence.

'I'm – I'm most awfully sorry,' he said, smiling at the girl's hat. 'But I can't go on sitting in the same carriage with you and not explaining why I dashed in like that, without my hat even. I'm sure I gave you a fright, and just now I was staring at you – but that's only an awful fault of mine; I'm a terrible starer! If you'd like me to explain – how I got in here – not about the staring, of course', – he gave a little laugh – 'I will'.

For a minute she said nothing, then in a low, shy voice – 'It doesn't matter.'

The train had flung behind the roofs and chimneys. They were swinging into the country, past little black woods and fading fields and pools of water shining under an apricot evening sky. Henry's heart began to thump and beat to the beat of the train. He couldn't leave it like that. She sat so quiet, hidden in her fallen hair. He felt that it was absolutely necessary that she should look up and understand him – understand him at least. He leant forward and clasped his hands round his knees.

'You see I'd just put all my things – a portfolio – into a third-class "smoker" and was having a look at the bookstall', he explained.

As he told the story she raised her head. He saw her grey eyes under the shadow of her hat and her eyebrows like two gold feathers. Her lips were faintly parted. Almost unconsciously he seemed to absorb the fact that she was wearing a bunch of primroses and that her throat was white – the shape of her face wonderfully delicate against all that burning hair. 'How beautiful she is! How simply beautiful she is!' sang Henry's heart, and swelled with the words, bigger and bigger and trembling like a marvellous bubble – so that he was afraid to breathe for fear of breaking it.

'I hope there was nothing valuable in the portfolio', said she, very grave.

'Oh, only some silly drawing that I was taking back from the office' answered Henry airily. 'And – I was rather glad to lose my hat. It had been hurting me all day.'

'Yes', she said, 'it's left a mark', and she nearly smiled.

Why on earth should those words have made Henry feel so free suddenly and so happy and so madly excited? What was happening between them? They said nothing, but to Henry their silence was alive and warm. It covered him from his head to his feet in a trembling wave. Her marvellous words, 'It's made a mark', had in some mysterious fashion established a bond between them. They could not be utter strangers to each other if she spoke so simply and so naturally. And now she was really smiling. The smile danced in her eyes, crept over her cheeks to her lips and stayed there. He leant back. The words flew from him – 'Isn't life wonderful!'

At that moment the train dashed into a tunnel. He heard her voice raised against the noise. She leant forward.

'I don't think so. But then I've been a fatalist for a long time now' – a pause – 'months.'

They were shattering through the dark. 'Why?' called Henry.

'Oh –'

Then she shrugged, and smiled and shook her head, meaning she could not speak against the noise. He nodded and leant back. They came out of the tunnel into a sprinkle of lights and houses. He waited for her to explain. But she got up and buttoned her coat and put her hands to her hat, swaying a little. 'I get out here,' she said. That seemed quite impossible to Henry.

The train slowed down and the lights outside grew brighter. She moved towards his end of the carriage.

'Look here!' he stammered. 'Shan't I see you again?' He got up too, and leant against the rack with one hand. 'I *must* see you again.' The train was stopping.

She said breathlessly, 'I come down from London every evening.'

'You – you – you do – really?' His eagerness frightened her. He was quick to curb it. Shall we or shall we not shake hands? raced through his brain. One hand was on the door-handle, the other held the little bag. The train stopped. Without another word or glance she was gone.

KATHERINE MANSFIELD (1888–1923)
Something Childish but Very Natural

There is no greater wonder than the way the face of a young woman fits in a man's mind, and stays there, and he could never tell you why; it just seems it was the thing he wanted.

ROBERT LOUIS STEVENSON (1850–1894)
Catriona

'Bill, are you really fond of me?'

'Fond of you!'

She gave a sigh. 'You're so splendid!'

Bill was staggered. Those were strange words. He had never thought much of himself. He had always looked on himself as rather a chump – well-meaning, perhaps, but an awful ass! It seemed incredible that anyone, and Elizabeth of all people, could look on him as splendid.

And yet the very fact that she had said it gave it a plausible sort of sound. It shook his convictions. Splendid! Was he? By Jove, perhaps he was, what? Rum idea, but it grew on a chap. Filled with a novel feeling of exaltation, he kissed Elizabeth eleven times in rapid succession.

He felt devilish fit. He would have liked to run a mile or two and jump a few gates. He felt grand and strong and full of beans. What a ripping thing life was when you came to think of it.

P. G. Wodehouse (1881–1975)
Uneasy Money

No disguise can long conceal love, where it exists, or long feign it where it is lacking.

La Rochefoucauld (1613–1680)
Maxims

Do you love me, Vic?' she says, and I put my face down in her neck where she can't see it. All I want now is to get away from her because I feel as lousy as I ever did about it all. And to think not an hour ago I didn't know where to put myself I was so mad for her.

Stan Barstow (born 1928)
A Kind of Loving

Dearest Hetty,
I have spoken truly when I have said that I loved you, and I shall never forget our love. . . . If I say anything to pain you in this letter, do not believe it is for want of love and tenderness towards you. . . . I cannot bear to think of my little Hetty shedding tears when I am not there to kiss them away; and if I followed my own inclinations, I should be with her at this moment instead of writing. . . .

Dear, dear Hetty, sweet as our love has been to me. . . . I feel that it would have been better for us both if we had never had that happiness, and that it is my duty to ask you to love me and care for me as little as you can. The fault has all been mine, for though I have been unable to resist the longing to be near you, I have felt all the while that your affection for me might cause you grief. I ought to have resisted my feelings. . . . For, dear Hetty, if I were to do what you one day spoke of, and make you my wife, I should do what you yourself would come to feel was for your misery instead of your welfare. I know you can never be happy except by marrying a man in your own station; and if I were to marry you now. I should only be adding to any wrong I have done, besides offending against my duty in the other relations of life. . . .

And since I cannot marry you, we must part – we must try not to feel like lovers any more. . . . Be angry with me, my sweet one, I deserve it; but do not believe that I shall not always care for you. . . .

Forgive me, and try to forget everything about me, except that I shall be, as long as I live, your affectionate friend.

Arthur Donnithorne

GEORGE ELIOT (1819–1880)
Adam Bede

One grows weary of everything, my angel, it is a law of Nature, it is not my fault.

If therefore I am weary today of an adventure which has wholly preoccupied me for four mortal months, it is not my fault.

If, for example, I had just as much love as you had virtue (and that is surely saying a lot) it is not astonishing that one should end at the same time as the other. It is not my fault.

From this it follows that for some time I have been deceiving you; but then your pitiless affection forced me as it were, to do so! It is not my fault.

I realize that this is a fine opportunity of crying out upon perjury; but if Nature has only given men assurance, while she gave women obstinacy, it is not my fault.

Take my advice, choose another love, as I have chosen another mistress. This is good advice, very good; if you think it bad, it is not my fault.

Farewell, my angel, I took you with pleasure, I abandon you without regret; perhaps I shall come back to you. So goes the world. It is not my fault.

CHODERLOS DE LACLOS (1741–1803)
Les Liaisons Dangereuses
(translated by Richard Aldington)

I remember the way we parted,
  The day and the way we met;
You hoped we were both broken-hearted,
  And knew we should both forget.

And the best and the worst of this is
  That neither is most to blame,
If you have forgotten my kisses
  And I have forgotten your name.

ALGERNON CHARLES SWINBURNE (1837–1909)
An Interlude

Summer

Getting married is a serious matter for a girl; not getting married is even more serious.

NICOLAS BENTLEY (born 1907)

To-day Otto asked me for a keepsake.
I offered him one of my hatpins. But he said no.
He has taken instead the diamond buckle from my belt.
I read his meaning.
He means that I am to him as a diamond is to lesser natures.

This Morning
Yesterday Otto asked me for another keepsake. I took a gold rouble from my bag and said that he should break it in half and that each should keep one of the halves.
But Otto said no. I divined his thoughts. It would violate our love to break the coin.
He is to keep it for both of us, and it is to remain unbroken like our love.
Is it not a sweet thought?
Otto is so thoughtful. He thinks of everything.
Today he asked me if I had another gold rouble.

Next Day
To-day I brought Otto another gold rouble.
His eyes shone with love when he saw it.
He has given me for it a bronze kopek. Our love is to be as pure as gold and as strong as bronze.
Is it not beautiful?

STEPHEN LEACOCK (1869–1944)
Nonsense Novels

A fool and knave with different views,
For Julia's hand apply:
The knave, to mend his fortune sues,
The fool, to please his eye.

Ask you, how Julia will behave?
Depend on't for a rule,
If she's a fool, she'll wed the knave –
If she's a knave, the fool.

S. BISHOP (born 1906)
The Maiden's Choice

In villages in Pakistan, a prospective bridegroom is brought before relatives of the bride, who insult him with every known invective. The theory is that, if he can take that, he has nothing to fear from what the bride will say later.

Suitors are dealt with tactfully in parts of Bosnia and Herzegovina. The young man is wined and dined by the girl's family, and all aspects of the prospective marriage are talked over. But the girl's family doesn't come out with a flat yes or no. Instead, at the end of the discussion, they serve coffee. If it is sweet, the suitor knows he has been accepted. If bitter – well, better luck elsewhere.

In every village once in each year it was done as follows. When the maidens grew to the age for marriage, they . . . brought them in a body to one place, and round them stood a company of men: and the crier caused each one severally to stand up, and proceeded to sell them first the most comely of all, and afterwards . . . the most comely after her. . . .

Now all the wealthy men of the Babylonians who were ready to marry vied with one another in bidding for the most beautiful maidens; those however of the common sort who were ready to marry did not require a fine form, but they would accept money together with less comely maidens.

HERODOTUS (5th century BC)
History

Marriage is a ghastly public confession of a strictly private intention.

IAN HAY (1876–1952)

Marriage: A sort of friendship recognized by the police.

ROBERT LOUIS STEVENSON (1850–1894)

Marriage is the only adventure open to the cowardly.

VOLTAIRE (1694–1778)

My dear Wormwood,

You must have learned at college the routine technique of sexual temptation, and since, for us spirits, this whole subject is one of considerable tedium (though necessary as part of our training) I will pass it over. But on the larger issues involved I think you have a good deal to learn. . . .

The Enemy's real motive for fixing on sex as the method of reproduction among humans is only too apparent from the use He has made of it. Sex might have been, from our point of view, quite innocent. It might have been merely one more mode in which a stronger self preyed upon a weaker – as it is, indeed, among the spiders where the bride concludes her nuptials by eating her groom. But in the humans the Enemy has gratuitously associated affection with sexual desire. . . . The whole thing, in fact, turns out to be simply one more device for dragging in Love.

Now comes the joke. The Enemy described a married couple as 'one flesh'. He did not say a 'happily married couple' or 'a couple who married because they were in love'; but you can make the humans ignore that. . . . You can . . . get the humans to accept as rhetorical eulogies of 'being in love' what were in fact plain descriptions of the real significance of sexual intercourse. . . .

Humans who have not the gift of continence can be deterred from seeking marriage as a solution because they do not find themselves 'in love', and, thanks to us, the idea of marrying with any other motive seems to them low and cynical. Yes, they think that. . . .

Any sexual infatuation whatever, so long as it intends marriage, will be regarded as 'love', and 'love' . . . will protect him from all the consequences, of marrying a heathen, a fool, or a wanton.

Your affectionate uncle
Screwtape

C. S. Lewis (1898–1963)
The Screwtape Letters

If I were able to give girls only one sentence of advice as to how to keep their husbands in love with them, I should choose this one – never revolt the man's senses.

A man will go on being in love with even a stupid woman who never fails to please his eye and his ear – whereas he will lose all emotion for the cleverest who revolts either.

ELINOR GLYN (1864–1943)
Points of View

Never mind the pieces of needlework, the tambouring, the maps of the world made by her needle. Get to see her at work upon a mutton-chop or a bit of bread and cheese and if she deal quickly with these, you have a pretty good security for that activity, that stirring industry, without which a wife is a burden instead of a help. And as to love, it cannot live for more than a month or two (in the breast of a man of spirit) towards a lazy woman. Another mark of industry is a quick step and a somewhat heavy tread, and if the body lean a little forward, and the eye keep steadily in the same direction while the feet are going, so much the better, for these discover earnestness to arrive at the intended point. I do not like, and I never liked, young, sauntering, soft-stepped girls who move as if they were perfectly indifferent to the result.

WILLIAM COBBETT (1762–1835)
Advice to Young Men

MRS SULLEN: If ever you marry, beware of a sullen, silent sot, one that's always musing, but never thinks. There's some diversion in a talking blockhead; and since a woman must wear chains, I would have the pleasure of hearing 'em rattle a little Now you shall see – but take this by the way: he came home this morning at his usual hour of four, wakened me out of a sweet dream of something else, by tumbling over the tea-table, which he broke all to pieces; after his man and he had rolled about the room like sick passengers in a storm, he comes flounce into bed, dead as a salmon into fishmonger's basket; his feet cold as ice, his breath hot as a furnace, and his hands and his face as greasy as his flannel nightcap. O matrimony! He tosses up the clothes with a barbarous swing over his shoulders, disorders the whole economy of my bed, leaves me half naked, and my whole night's comfort is the tuneable serenade of that wakeful nightingale, his nose! Oh, the pleasure of counting the melancholy clock by a snoring husband!

GEORGE FARQUHAR (1678–1707)
The Beaux' Stratagem

My Dear Friend,

I know of no medicine fit to diminish the violent nocturnal inclinations you mention, and if I did, I think I should not communicate it to you. Marriage is the proper remedy. . . .

But if you will not take this counsel, and persist in thinking commerce with the sex inevitable, then I repeat my former advice, that in your amours you should prefer *old women to young ones*. You call this a paradox, and demand reasons. They are these:

First: Because they have more knowledge of the World. . . . and their conversation is more lastingly agreeable.

Second: Because when women cease to be handsome they study to be good. . . . They learn to do a thousand services, small and great, and are the most tender and useful of all friends when you are sick. . . . Thus they continue amiable, and hence there is scarcely such a thing to be found as an old woman who is not a good woman.

Third: Because there is no hazard of children, which irregularly produced, may be attended with much inconvenience.

Fourth: Because, through more experience, they are more prudent and discreet in conducting an intrigue to prevent suspicion. . . . If the affair should happen to be known, considerate people might be rather inclined to excuse an old woman who would kindly take care of a young man . . . and prevent his ruining his health and fortune among mercenary prostitutes.

Fifth: Because in every animal that walks upright the deficiency of the fluid that fills the muscles appear but on the highest part. The face first grows lank and wrinkled, then the neck. . . . As in the dark all cats are grey, the pleasure of corporal enjoyment with an old woman is at least equal and frequently superior; every knack being, by practice, capable of improvement.

Sixth: Because the sin is less. The debauching a virgin may be her ruin and make her life unhappy.

Seventh: Because the compunction is less. The having made a young girl miserable may give you frequent bitter reflections, none of which can attend making an old woman happy.

Eight and lastly: They are so grateful....

Your affectionate friend,
B. Franklin

BENJAMIN FRANKLIN (1706–1790)
Letter written to a young man in 1745

Marriage: A ceremony in which rings are put on the finger of the lady and through the nose of the gentleman.

HERBERT SPENCER (1820–1903)

It isn't tying himself to one woman that a man dreads when he thinks of marrying; it's separating himself from all the others.

HELEN ROWLAND

Marriage is popular because it combines the maximum of temptation with the maximum of opportunity.

GEORGE BERNARD SHAW (1856–1950)

Marriage is like a cage; one sees the birds outside desperate to get in and those inside equally desperate to get out.

MICHEL MONTAIGNE (1533–1592)

This letter comes to know whether you will be pleased to give me leave to propose marriage to your daughter, Miss Elizabeth. You need not be afraid of sending me a refusal; for I bless God, if I know anything of my own heart, I am free from that foolish passion which the world calls love.

GEORGE WHITEFIELD (1714–1770)

Princess Victoria Louise had declared when she was still in the school room that she would only marry for love, and when her father, the Emperor, tried to explain to her that in Royal houses one could not do all that is allowed to simpler mortals, the girl merely shrugged her shoulders, and replied that in the twentieth century even princesses had the right to please themselves in the choice of a husband. . . .

When she had passed her twentieth birthday and had refused several brilliant matches one after another, amongst them the hand of the then hereditary Grand Duke of Mecklenburg-Strelitz, the Emperor thought it time to display his diplomatic strategy. . . . On more than one occasion he had been in Munich and had had the opportunity of making the acquaintance of Prince Ernest Augustus, son of the Duke of Cumberland. The young man had met with his approval. He had found him unaffected, simple in his tastes and manners, and admirably well brought up. His political opinions appeared to the critical eyes of the anxious father to be sound . . . So Prince Ernest took the hint that was given him, and ventured to express to the Emperor the timid hope that he would be allowed to pay his attentions to the Princess Victoria Louise.

The Emperor, however, was far too wise to invite the Prince to begin his courtship in Berlin, where his arrival would inevitably excite his daughter to discourage her would-be suitor. He therefore sought the help of the Crown Princess, Cecile, whom the doctors had ordered to St Moritz for the winter, and asked her to take her young sister-in-law with her. . . . The Crown Princess entered into the conspiracy with zest . . . and begged Victoria Louise to accompany her.

At St Moritz the two princesses entered heartily into the winter sports, and when, as if by chance, Prince Ernest arrived, he naturally saw a lot of them. . . .

It was not long before the daughter of the German Emperor, suspecting nothing, became aware of a more than passing interest in Ernest Augustus. . . . She immediately began to plan by what means she could induce her father to agree to let her marry him, as she was sure the Emperor would consider the idea monstrous.

Meanwhile the Crown Princess chided her sister-in-law for getting too friendly with Prince Ernest. . . . This was enough to make Victoria Louise declare that she . . . would never marry anyone else. . . .

There were stormy scenes . . . Victoria Louise had scarcely alighted from the train at the railway station in Berlin, where her father met her on her return, when she herself broached the subject of her attachment, and begged the Emperor's consent.

Of course, the Emperor began by objecting, and allowed a few months to pass under the pretext of political difficulties, before at last he gave his consent. . . . He did not care for his daughter to suspect that this husband, whom she was so delighted to have chosen for herself in face of so much opposition, had really been the one whom, for years, her father had wished her to marry.

COUNT AXEL VON SCHWERING
The Berlin Court under William II

We pledged our hearts, my love and I,
  I in my arms the maiden clasping;
I could not tell the reason why,
  But oh! I trembled like an aspen.

Her father's love she bade me gain;
  I went, and shook like any reed;
I strove to act the man – in vain!
  We had exchanged our hearts indeed.

SAMUEL TAYLOR COLERIDGE (1772–1834)
The Exchange

'Come, come,' said Tom's father, 'at your time of life,
  There's no longer excuse for thus playing the rake –
It is time, you should think, boy, of taking a wife.'
  'Why so it is, father, pray whose shall I take?'

THOMAS MOORE (1779–1852)

About this time Sir William Miller, a friend of the family, suggested to my parents that his eldest son – a charming young fellow since dead – should marry me. . . . We were invited to stay at Manderston, much to my father's delight.

On the evening of our arrival my host said to me in his broad Scottish accent:

'Margy, will you marry my son Jim?'

'My dear Sir William', I replied, 'your son Jim has never spoken to me in his life!'

SIR WILLIAM: 'He is shy.'

I assured him that this was not so and that I thought his son might be allowed to choose for himself, adding:

'You are like my father, Sir William, and think everyone wants to marry.'

SIR WILLIAM: 'So they do, don't they?' (with a sly look) 'I am sure they all want to marry you.'

MARGOT: 'I wonder!'

SIR WILLIAM: 'Margy, would you rather marry me or break your leg?'

MARGOT: 'Break both, Sir William.'

MARGOT ASQUITH (1864–1945)
Autobiography

The surest way to hit a woman's heart is to take aim kneeling.

DOUGLAS JERROLD (1803–1857)

On Monday evening Mr Nicholls was here to tea. I vaguely felt without clearly seeing, as without seeing I have felt for some time, the meaning of his constant looks, and strange, feverish restraint. . . . He stopped in the passage, he tapped: like lightning it flashed on me what was coming. . . . What his words were you can guess; his manner – you can hardly realize – never can I forget it. Shaking from head to foot, looking deadly pale, speaking low, vehemently yet with difficulty – he made me for the first time feel what it costs a man to declare affection where he doubts response.

The spectacle of one ordinarily so statue-like, thus trembling, stirred and overcome, gave me a kind of strange shock. He spoke of sufferings he had borne for months, of sufferings he could endure no longer, and craved leave for some hope. I could only entreat him to leave me then and promise a reply on the morrow.

CHARLOTTE BRONTË (1816–1855)
Letters

Open and obvious devotion from any sort of man is always pleasing to any sort of woman.

RUDYARD KIPLING (1865–1936)
Plain Tales from the Hills

He that would the daughter win, must with the mother first begin.

[*Crosbie jilted Mrs Dale's daughter, Lily, in order to marry money and a title. Although she still loves him Lily refuses to see Crosbie again.*]

Madam,

You will be very much surprised to hear from me, and I am quite aware that I am not entitled to the ordinary courtesy of an acknowledgement from you....

I will only refer to that episode of my life with which you are acquainted, for the sake of acknowledging my great fault and of assuring you that I did not go unpunished. . . . I will ask you to believe that my folly was greater than my sin.

You are, no doubt, aware that I married a daughter of Lady de Courcy, and that I was separated from my wife a few weeks after our unfortunate marriage. It is now something over twelve months since she died at Baden-Baden in her mother's house. I never saw her since the daywe were first parted. . . . The fault was mine in marrying a woman whom I did not love and had never loved. When I married Lady Alexandrina I loved, not her, but your daughter.

I believe I may venture to say that your daughter once loved me. From the day on which I last wrote to you that terrible letter which told you of my fate, I have never mentioned the name of Lily Dale to human ears. It has been too sacred for my mouth – too sacred for the intercourse of any friendship with which I have been blessed. I now use it for the first time to you, in order that I may ask whether it be possible that her old love should ever live again. Mine has lived always – has never faded for an hour. . . .

If you can tell me that there can be a gleam of hope, I will obey any commands that you can put upon me in any way that you may point out. I am free again – and she is free. I love her with all my heart, and seem to long for nothing in the world but that she should become my wife. Whether any of her old love may still abide with her, you will know. If it do, it may even yet prompt her to forgive one who, in spite of falseness of conduct, has yet been true to her in heart – I have the honour to be, madam, your most obedient servant,

Adolphus Crosbie

ANTHONY TROLLOPE (1815–1882)
Last Chronicle of Barset

I have moreover read your letter. For *it* I do *not* thank you. It afforded me neither pleasure nor amusement. Indeed, my Friend, this letter of yours has, to my mind, more than one fault. I do not allude to its being egotistical. To speak of oneself is, they say, a privilege of Friendship. . . . There is about your Letter a *mystery* which I detest. It is so full of *meaning* words underlined, *meaning* sentences half finished; *meaning* blanks with notes of admiration; and *meaning* quotations from foreign languages, that really in this abundance of meaning . . . I am somewhat at a loss to discover what you would be at. I know how you will excuse yourself on this score: you will say that you knew my Mother would see your Letter; and that, of course, you cared not what difficulties I as interpreter might be subjected to, so that you got your feelings towards me expressed. Now, Sir, once and for all, I beg you to understand that *I dislike* as much as my *Mother disapproves* your somewhat too ardent expressions of friendship towards me; and that if you cannot write to me as to a man who feels a deep interest in your welfare, who admires your talents, respects your virtues, and for the sake of these has often – perhaps too often – overlooked your faults; if you cannot write to me as if – as if you were married, you need never waste ink or paper on me more.

JANE WELSH (1801–1866)
Letter to Thomas Carlyle (1795–1881), 1822

[*Four years later, in 1826, Jane Welsh married Thomas Carlyle. Women !*]

I have always thought that every woman should marry, and no man.

BENJAMIN DISRAELI, Earl of Beaconsfield (1804–1881)

Love makes marriage possible; habit makes it endurable.

If it were not for the presents, an elopement would be preferable.

GEORGE ADE (1866–1944)

In love with his neighbour's daughter, Mr Dorsun Yilmaz of Dalmali, Yugoslavia, organized an elopement.

Soon after midnight, his beloved, wrapped in a blanket, descended the ladder he had placed by her window. He carried her to the car and away they sped.

Five miles down the road he unwrapped his treasure, and found that he was carrying the girl's grandmother, who beat him up.

The Sun
26 August 1972

Aunt Stella eloped when she was sixteen with a well-known Bavarian artist, Alexander Svoboda. My grandfather would not tolerate this love affair, and he must, I think, have locked her into a room, for we were told she escaped by climbing up the wide chimney of a Moorish house, her sisters helping her to drag up a box by a rope. I take it she was successfully helped down into the street, where Svoboda was waiting for her. . . .

The marriage was not happy; Svoboda was intensely jealous. Aunt Stella had a bird, which used to feed from her lips. One day this infuriated Svoboda . . . in a fit of jealousy, wrung the bird's neck before her eyes. . . .

My Aunt Stella died at twenty-nine, leaving behind her just this little sequence: her beauty, her young love, her escape up the chimney, her bird killed to spite her, and her early death.

MRS PATRICK CAMPBELL (1865–1940)
My Life and Some Letters

Thus grief still treads upon
The heels of pleasure;
Married in haste, we may
Repent at leisure.

WILLIAM CONGREVE (1670–1729)

Why have such scores of lovely, gifted girls
  Married impossible men?
Simple self-sacrifice may be ruled out,
  And missionary endeavour, nine times out ten.

Repeat 'impossible men': not merely rustic,
  Foul-tempered or depraved
(Dramatic foils chosen to show the world
  How well women behave, and always have behaved).

Impossible men: idle, illiterate,
  Self-pitying, dirty, sly,
For whose appearance even in City parks
  Excuses must be made to casual passers-by.

Has God's supply of tolerable husbands
  Fallen, in fact, so low?
Or do I always over-value woman
  At the expense of Man?

    Do I?

        It might be so.

ROBERT GRAVES (born 1895)
A Slice of Wedding Cake

Being asked whether it was better to marry or not, Socrates replied, 'Whichever you do you will repent it.'

DIOGENES LAERTIUS (420–324 BC)

At long last I am able to say a few words of my own. I have never wanted to withhold anything, but until now it has not been constitutionally possible for me to speak.

A few hours ago I discharged my last duty as King and Emperor, and now that I have been succeeded by my brother, the Duke of York, my first words must be to declare my allegiance to him.

This I do with all my heart.

You all know the reasons which have impelled me to renounce the throne, but I want you to understand that in making up my mind I did not forget the country or the Empire, which as Prince of Wales and lately as King I have for twenty-five years tried to serve.

But you must believe me when I tell you that I have found it impossible to carry the heavy burden of responsibility and discharge my duties as King as I would wish to do without the help and support of the woman I love. . . .

King Edward VIII (1894–1974)
Abdication Speech
10 December 1936

There is nothing nobler or more admirable than when two people who see eye to eye keep house as man and wife, confounding their enemies and delighting their friends.

Homer (*c.* 900 BC)

Marriage resembles a pair of shears, so joined that they cannot be separated; often moving in opposite directions, yet always punishing anyone who comes between them.

Sydney Smith (1771–1845)

I look down the tracks and see you coming – and out of every haze and mist your darling rumpled trousers are hurrying to me – without you, dearest, dearest, I couldn't see or hear or feel or think – or live – I love you so and I'm never in all our lives going to let us be apart another night. It's like begging for mercy of a storm, or killing Beauty or growing old, without you. . . . Goofo, you've *got* to try to feel how much I love you – how inanimate I am when you're gone – I can't even hate these damnable people – nobody's got any right to live but us – and they're dirtying up our world and I can't hate them because I want you so. Come quick to me – I could never do without you if you hated me and were covered with sores like a leper – and if you ran away with another woman and starved and beat me – I still would want you – I still would want you *I know.*

ZELDA FITZGERALD (1900–1948)
Letter to Scott Fitzgerald (1896–1940)

Marriage: The state or condition of a community consisting of a master, a mistress, and two slaves, making in all two.

If, after all, you still will doubt and fear me,
  And think this heart to other loves will stray,
If I must swear, then, lovely doubter, hear me;
  By every dream I have when thou'rt away,
By every throb I feel when thou art near me,
  I love but thee – I love but thee!

By those dark eyes, where light is ever playing,
  Where Love, in depth of shadow, holds his throne,
And by those lips, which give whate'er thou'rt saying,
  Or grave or gay, a music of its own,
A music far beyond all minstrel's playing,
  I love but thee – I love but thee!

By that fair brow, where Innocence reposes,
  As pure as moonlight sleeping upon snow,
And by that cheek, whose fleeting blush discloses
  A hue too bright to bless this world below,
And only fit to dwell on Eden's roses,
  I love but thee – I love but thee!

THOMAS MOORE (1779–1852)
I Love But Thee

[*The wedding of Czar Nicholas* II *and Princess Alix of Hesse-Darmstadt took place on 26 November 1894.*]

The marriage that began that night remained unflawed for the rest of their lives. It was a Victorian marriage, outwardly serene and proper, but based on intensely passionate physical love. On her wedding night, before going to bed, Alexandra wrote in her husband's diary: 'At last united, bound for life, and when this life is ended, we meet again in the other world and remain together for eternity. Yours, yours'. The next morning, with fresh, new emotions surging through her, she wrote, 'Never did I believe there could be such utter happiness in this world, such a feeling of unity between two mortal beings. I love you, those three words have my life in them'.

ROBERT K. MASSIE (born 1929)
Nicholas and Alexandra

[*Letter from Czar Nicholas* II (*1868–1918*) *to the Czarina Alexandra* (*1872–1918*)].

My Precious Darling,

My warm and loving thanks for your dear letter, full of tender words, and for both telegrams. I too have you in my thoughts on this our 21st anniversary! I wish you health and all that a deeply loving heart can desire, and thank you on my knees for all your love, affection, friendship and patience, which you have shown me during these long years of our married life!

Today's weather reminds me of that day in Coburg – *how sad it is that we are not together!* Nobody knew that it was the day of our betrothal – it is strange how soon people forget – besides, it means nothing to them. . . .

Before the evening I drove along the old road to the town of Slonin in the province of Grodno. It was extraordinarily warm and pleasant; and the smell of the pine forest – one feels enervated and softened!

Always your hubby,
Nicky

Feb. 7th (Lord's Day). I up, and go to church, and so home to dinner, where my wife in a jealous fit, which lasted all the afternoon, and shut herself up in her closet, and I mightily grieved and vexed, and could not get her to tell me what ailed her, or to let me into her closet, but at last she did, where I found her crying on the ground and could not please her; but at last find that she did plainly expound it to me. It was, that she did believe me false to her with Jane, and did rip up three or four silly circumstances of her not rising till I come out of my chamber, and her letting me thereby see her dressing herself; and that I must needs go into her chamber; which was so silly, and so far from truth, that I could not be troubled at it, though I could not wonder at her being troubled if she had these thoughts. At last, I did give her such satisfaction, that we were mighty good friends.

SAMUEL PEPYS (1633–1703)
Diary

... Life is quite a different thing by the side of a beloved wife. ... Beautiful Nature! I now for the first time fully enjoy it, live in it. The world again clothes itself around me in poetic forms; old feelings are again awakening in my breast. ... My existence is settled in harmonious composure – not strained and impassioned, but peaceful and clear. I look to my future destiny with a cheerful heart; now when standing at the wished-for goal, I wonder with myself, how it has all happened so far beyond my expectations. Fate has conquered the difficulties for me. ... From the future I expect everything. ...

FRIEDRICH SCHILLER (1759–1805)
(after his marriage)

How do I love thee ? Let me count the ways.
I love thee to the depth and breadth and height
My soul can reach, when feeling out of sight
For the ends of Being and ideal Grace.
I love thee to the level of every day's
Most quiet need, by sun and candlelight.
I love thee freely, as men strive for Right;
I love thee purely, as they turn from Praise.
I love thee with the passion put to use
In my old griefs, and with my childhood's faith.
I love thee with a love I seemed to lose
With my lost saints, – I love thee with the breath,
Smiles, Tears, of all my life! – and, if God choose,
I shall but love thee better after death.

ELIZABETH BARRETT BROWNING (1806–1861)
Sonnets from the Portuguese (XLIII)

Why, having won her, do I woo?
  Because her spirit's vestal grace
Provokes me always to pursue,
  But, spirit-like, eludes embrace;
Because her womanhood is such
  That, as on court-days subjects kiss
The Queen's hand, yet so near a touch
  Affirms no mean familiarness;
Nay, rather marks more fair the height
  Which can with safety so neglect
To dread, as lower ladies might,
  That grace could meet with disrespect;
Thus she with happy favour feeds
  Allegiance from a love so high
That thence no false conceit proceeds
  Of difference bridged, or state put by;

Because although in act and word
  As lovely as a wife can be,
Her manners, when they call me lord,
  Remind me 'tis by courtesy;
Not with her least consent of will,
  Which would my proud affection hurt,
But by the noble style that still
  Imputes an unattain'd desert;
Because her gay and lofty brows,
  When all is won which hope can ask,
Reflect a light of hopeless snows,
  That bright in virgin ether bask;
Because, though free of the outer court
  I am, this Temple keeps its shrine
Sacred to Heaven; because, in short,
  She's not and never can be mine.

COVENTRY PATMORE (1823–1896)
The Married Lover

Autumn

There are two tragedies in life.
One is not to get your heart's desire.
The other is to get it.

GEORGE BERNARD SHAW (1856–1950)

Your little hands,
Your little feet,
Your little mouth –
Oh, God, how sweet!

Your little nose,
Your little ears,
Your eyes, that shed
Such little tears!

Your little voice,
So soft and kind;
Your little soul,
Your little mind!

SAMUEL HOFFENSTEIN (1890–1947)
Your Little Hands

I spent two weeks with my wife in Moscow. Those two weeks were a series of the most unbearable mental agonies. I saw right away that I could never love my wife, and that the *habit* on which I had counted would never come. I fell into despair and longed for death, which seemed the only way out. I had moments of madness in which my whole being was filled with such terrific distaste for my poor wife that I wanted to strangle her. I could not carry on my work either in the Conservatory or at home. My mind began to go. Yet I knew I alone was to blame. My wife, whatever she may be, is not responsible for my encouraging her and bringing us to the point of marriage. My lack of character, my weakness, blundering and childishness were responsible for everything.

PETER TCHAIKOVSKY (1840–1893)
Letter to Nadejda Philaretovna

Love doesn't grow on the trees like apples in Eden – it's something you have to make. And you have to use your imagination to make it, too, just like anything else. It's all work, work.

JOYCE CARY (1888–1957)

Love does not consist in gazing at each other but in looking outward together in the same direction.

ANTOINE DE ST-EXUPÉRY (1900–1944)

Many a man in love with a dimple makes the mistake of marrying the whole girl.

A husband is a man who, two minutes after his head touches the pillow, is snoring like an overloaded omnibus.

OGDEN NASH (1902–1971)

Woman begins by resisting man's advances and ends by blocking his retreat.

Before marriage a man will lie awake all night thinking about something you said; after marriage, he'll fall asleep before you finish saying it.

HELEN ROWLAND

My notion of a wife at forty is that a man should be able to change her, like a banknote, for two twenties.

DOUGLAS JERROLD (1803–1857)

Twenty years of romance make a woman look like a ruin; but twenty years of marriage make her something like a public building.

OSCAR WILDE (1854–1900)

My wife has a whim of iron.

OLIVER HERFORD (1863–1935)

No man can constantly sleep with his wife and take heartfelt pleasure in it.

NICARCHUS (1st century AD)

When an Englishman can't get on with his wife, he goes to his club. A Frenchman goes to his mistress. An American goes to his lawyer.

English women assume their husbands will be loyal. American women assume their husbands are loyal. French women assume their husbands will be home for dinner.

FRED SPARKS (born 1915)

After dinner . . . the food inside him and the warmth of the room combined to send him to sleep in five minutes, and there he sprawled, with his chin on his hands, his shock of hair flopping down over the lamp-stand. Emma looked at him and shrugged her shoulders. Why hadn't she at any rate one of those silent, earnest husbands who work at their books all night – and end up, by the time that rheumatism sets in at sixty, wearing a string of decorations on their ill-fitting dress-coats! She would have liked this name of Bovary, that was hers, to be famous, on view at the bookshops, always cropping up in the papers, known all over France. But Charles had no ambition. . . .

She was getting generally more irritated with him. As he grew older he became grosser in his ways. He used to whittle down the corks of the empty bottles during dessert. He sucked his teeth after eating. When he drank soup he made a gulping noise at every mouthful. And now that he had begun to put on weight, his puffy cheeks seemed to be pushing eyes, which had always been small, right up to his temples.

Emma used sometimes to tuck the red border of his undervest inside his waistcoat, or straighten his cravat, or throw away a shabby pair of gloves that he was about to put on. She did these things not, as he imagined, for his sake, but for her own, in an outburst of egoism, a nervous irritation. And sometimes she told him what she had been reading – a passage in a novel, a new play, or a bit of society gossip retailed in her paper. Charles was someone to talk to, after all – an ever-open ear, an ever-ready approbation. She confided quite enough in her greyhound! She would have confided in the logs in the fireplace, or the pendulum of the clock.

And all the time, deep within her, she was waiting for something to happen. . . .

GUSTAVE FLAUBERT (1821–1880)
Madame Bovary

By the time you swear you're his,
Shivering and sighing,
And he vows his passion is
Infinite, undying –
Lady, make a note of this,
One of you is lying.

DOROTHY PARKER (1893–1967)

When one is in love one always begins by deceiving oneself, and one always ends by deceiving others. That is what the world calls a romance.

OSCAR WILDE (1854–1900)

Never ask your husband questions. If you do, you may be certain he will only tell you the truth when he feels inclined – and one day you will find this out, and then think he is always lying.

ELINOR GLYN (1864–1943)

With a man, a lie is a last resort; with woman, it's First Aid.

GELETT BURGESS (1866–1951)

SHE: If to demands of others I agree,
Then I will be another, but not me.

HE: If their requiring voices shake your ear,
How will your very spirit help but hear?

SHE: It will, a bird, desert its builded nest,
And in the virgin cloudbank only rest.

HE: If they have wings like other birds of prey,
How will it from those ruptors keep away?

SHE: It will seek out the ocean's whitest curl,
And sink within it and become a pearl.

HE: But when they dive as glittering fishers dive,
Will they not take your luster all alive?

SHE: Venue shall make no difference to disguise,
Nor shall my center open to their eyes.

HE: But if by chance, by force, by God knows how,
You all unguarded should some night allow
Another there beside you in your bed,
Body is body, and will not lie dead.

SHE: Body is body, but the heart stays true,
And should that happen, I will think him you.

WILLIAM DICKEY (born 1928)
Resolving Doubts

Make love to every woman you meet; if you get five per cent on your outlays it's a good investment.

ARNOLD BENNETT (1867–1931)

If you cannot inspire a woman with love of yourself, fill her above the brim with love of herself; all that runs over will be yours.

C. C. COLTON (1780–1852)

Thy leopard legs & python thighs,
Thy perched breasts & darting eyes,

Thy growling belly in its lair,
Thy crafty copperhead of hair,

Thy silky calves & furry groins,
Thy maney, rippling lion-loins,

Thy hind-behind – all these pursue
In beastly order (& I too)

The Pussy's primitive purlieu:
Unlock, unlock! Let's feed thy zoo.

ARTHUR FREEMAN (born 1938)
The Zoo of You

A famous concert pianist was asked if he felt lonely during a tour of one-night-only performances. Not at all, he replied. He resorts to a never-failing trick to assure himself of pleasant company. 'After each concert', he said, 'people line up backstage to congratulate me. When I see an attractive lady waiting, I rip a button off my waistcoat. Then, when she congratulates me, I say to her modestly, 'What good is it all? I haven't even got anyone to sew a button on.' Invariably she volunteers, and stays.

LEONARD LYON (born 1906)

The two divinest things a man has got;
A lovely woman in a rural spot.

LEIGH HUNT (1784–1859)

The two divinest things a man can grab;
A handsome woman in a hansom cab.

COVENTRY PATMORE (1823–1896)

They found a taxi. He took her home.
She spoke of her husband the while.
He knew she had power to charm him some.
He didn't as much as smile.

They rode down the midnight thoroughfare.
While somebody sat at the wheel.
The stars had painted their faces fair.
The streets were empty and still.

And when the taxi swung around curves,
Their knees just managed to touch.
And it was plainly a case of nerves,
Whenever it swung too much.

He recommended a show to see.
His manner was slightly forced.
She spoke of her lovely family.
Her voice sounded thin and lost.

And though he looked out of the window, he knew
That the gaze she gave him was steady.
And she was suddenly troubled too,
And thought, 'We are there already'.

Then both of them didn't speak for a space.
Above them the lightning broke.
The thing was awkward. He felt that the place
Was right for a funny joke.

The air was mild. And the taxi ran.
It galloped on faith and fuel.
They didn't think nature could do them a damn,
But rubbing knees was cruel.

So at last they got out. He gave her his hand.
And went. And left it at that.
Though later, at home in his room, he would stand
And kick a hole in his hat.

ERICH KÄSTNER (born 1899)
The Moral Taxi Ride
(translated from the German by Jerome Dennis Rothenberg)

The man she had was kind and clean
And well enough for every day,
But, oh, dear friends, you should have seen
The one who got away!

DOROTHY PARKER (1893–1967)
The Fisherwoman

Whether a woman always has her eyes fixed on the same person, or whether she persistently avoids looking at him one draws the same conclusion about her.

JEAN DE LA BRUYÈRE (1645–1696)

LORD FOPPINGTON: 'Tis a vast pleasure to receive encouragement from a woman before her husband's face.

JOHN VANBRUGH (1664–1726)
The Relapse

'Would you play something for me?' she whispered in a low, soft voice. 'Gladly,' I answered, and we went to the piano. Her husband stopped talking and settled himself comfortably on the little sofa, and she pushed one of the armchairs nearer to the piano.

'What will you play?' she asked, putting a vase with dark red roses on the side of the piano stand.

'Something of Chopin,' and I began to play the long D flat Nocturne as though in a trance, inspired by her beauty. The Count closed his eyes; when his chin dropped, a barely audible soft snore announced that he was asleep. When I reached the coda with its pianissimo descending sighs, the Countess, suddenly, leaned forward close to me and, covered by the open stand and the flowers, kissed my mouth with a wild passion. I struck a wrong note, too loudly – the Count woke up, and the charm was broken. We finished our champagne, I kissed her hand several times, with ardor; the Count accompanied me to the door, and I left the house. I never saw either of them again.

ARTHUR RUBINSTEIN (born 1888)
My Young Years

As I sat down by her side I dropped an arm round her waist and drawing her to my bosom I implored her to grant me her love – even to leave her husband and fly with me to some remote corner of the earth where we could while away our years in the soft dalliance of love.

I told her that her husband was an old man with whom a young woman like herself could not receive those tender attentions, and the soft and real pleasure which she could enjoy in the arms of a young and devoted lover.

She sighed and hung her head on her breast, saying she never knew what it was to receive those delicious and tender pleasures from her husband that I had just spoken of. That from the time of her marriage to the present moment, his whole time was taken up with drinking and gambling. That he left her to amuse herself as best she could in the house, for he was so jealous that he would never allow her to go out except in his company. She sighed again and wished that heaven had given her such a man as myself.

I know not how it was, but when she stopped, I found one of my hands had opened the front of her dress and slipped beneath her shift and was moulding one of her large hard breasts, and my lips were pressed on hers.

My leaning against her had insensibly moved her backwards till, without our knowing it, her head was resting on the cushion of the sofa and Iwas lying on top of her.

Whilst I was assuring her of eternal love and constancy and begging her to allow me to give her a convincing proof of my tenderness and affection, and also to let me convince her that as yet she had had the mere shadow of the ecstatic pleasure of love, but that if she would allow me I would give her the real substance and a surfeit of those pleasure of which I felt convinced she had received but a taste from her husband, I had been gradually drawing up her clothes, till my hand rested on a large, firm, fleshy thigh. Isabel had closed her eyes, her head hanging to one side, her lips slightly apart and her breast rising and falling rapidly from the quick pulsations of the blood caused by her fierce and amorous desires.

I raised her shift still higher till it disclosed to my sight a large tuft of long black hair. I then unbuttoned my pantaloons and with a little gentle force parted her legs, and got between her thighs.

La Rose D'Amour
or *The Adventures of a Gentleman in Search of Pleasure*
(translated from the French in the Victorian magazine *The Pearl*)

When a woman has an affair of the heart, she goes into ecstasies; a man goes into details.

Potemkin ordered Catherine's private life so efficiently that she was compelled to make her choice (of a lover) from among the candidates sent her by him, with his official sanction. . . . There were fifteen of them in all. . . . These favourites normally lasted for a period of two years, at the end of which time they temporarily disappeared from court, loaded with expensive presents. They were 'kept women'. . . . But when Catherine tired of her lovers, she no longer spent her nights weeping and her days moaning. It was all much simpler now. . . . The new favourite was generally petted, adored, praised to the skies and presented to the Empress's numerous correspondents as the model of all human perfections. He was paraded at Catherine's side to all official receptions, not openly acknowledged as her lover . . . but permanently on duty, expected to be absolutely faithful . . . and dismissed without ceremony when she no longer liked him.

ZOË OLDENBOURG (born 1916)
Catherine the Great

A beautiful woman once told her sullen, much-married looking lover: 'When you are seen, monsieur, in society with my husband, you are expected to look more cheerful than he does.'

SÉBASTIEN CHAMFORT (1740/41–1794)

It was when they had been married for two years that they got a new neighbour. . . . Jack Carr his name was. He was quite a different sort of chap from Norman; for one thing he was a gentleman, he'd been to a public school and a university; he was about thirty-five, tall, not beefy like Norman, but slight, he had the sort of figure that looked lovely in evening dress; and he had crisply curling hair and a laughing look in his eyes. Just her type. She took to him at once. . . .

It did not take her long to discover that Jack Carr wanted her. She was excited. She'd never been promiscuous, but in all those years she'd been on the stage naturally there'd been episodes. . . .

They understood one another all right, Jack and her; they knew it was bound to happen sooner or later, it was only a matter of waiting for the opportunity; and the opportunity came. But then something happened that they hadn't bargained for: they fell madly in love with one another. . . . They were two very ordinary people, he a jolly, good-natured, commonplace planter, and she a small-part actress far from clever, not even very young, with nothing to recommend her but a neat figure and a prettyish face. What started as a casual affair turned without warning into a devastating passion, and neither of them was of a texture to sustain its exorbitant compulsion. They longed to be with one another; they were restless and miserable apart. She'd been finding Norman a bore for some time, but she'd put up with him because he was her husband; now he irritated her to frenzy because he stood between her and Jack. . . . It was difficult for them to meet. They had to run awful risks. Perhaps the chances they had to take, the obstacles they had to surmount, were fuel to their love; a year passed and it was as overwhelming as at the beginning; it was a year of agony and bliss.

W. Somerset Maugham (1874–1965).
Flotsam and Jetsam

There is sanctuary in reading, sanctuary in formal society, in the company of old friends, and in the giving of officious help to strangers, but there is no sanctuary in one bed from the memory of another.

CYRIL CONNOLLY (1903–1974)

Oh, my lovely love, thought Madeline, my own sweet, husband whom I love with all my heart. How beautiful, how beautiful he looks in the dim lamplight, his dark brow, his grey eyes, his good jaw now slightly bearded at the end of the day, his delicate light fingers that have brought me so much pleasure lying curled up and easy on the arm of his chair as if begging me to put my hand in them. And how good he is. No, it doesn't matter how good he *is*; how good he tries to be, human good, not Sunday-school good. That's what matters. My sweet, dear husband. My darling, show-offy, gentle husband. My love.

Ah, Christ, he thought, staring at himself in the bathroom mirror, how can you ? How can you come out and face her ? And touch her and talk to her and sit with her at dinner and play the lovey-dovey spouse – when all the time the counterfeit is ringing inside you like a lead quarter. How can you keep it from showing ? You phoney. You low louse.

It would be different if you didn't have everything here, if you weren't happy. That would be some excuse. Every excuse maybe. But not this way.

Sometimes, he thought, I wish it were alcohol with me, instead of what it is. A drunk can't possibly hide it. He staggers, he gets a red nose. People have to know, and so they have to make a decision about him. Either to cut him off and despise him, or to help him. He can't deceive. The way I do. The way I keep doing, doing, doing.

. . . And desperately have to keep on doing, because if she ever found out . . . well, what would become of me without her?

STANLEY KAUFFMANN (born 1916)
The Philanderer

HESTER: I came up to the golf club to collect you to go on to that party at the Hendersons'. You were still out playing. Freddie was there alone. He'd been chucked for a game and was bad-tempered. I'd met him several times before up at the club with the others – but I'd never paid much attention to him. I didn't think he was even particularly good-looking, and the R.A.F. slang used to irritate me slightly, I remember. It's such an anachronism now, isn't it – as dated as gadzooks and odds my life. . . . Well – that day you were a long time over your game. . . . And Freddie and I sat on the veranda together for at least an hour. For some reason he talked very honestly and rather touchingly about himself – how worried he was about his future, how his life seemed to have no direction or purpose, how he envied you – the brilliant lawyer. . . . Then quite suddenly he put his hand on my arm and murmured something very conventional, about envying you for other reasons besides your career. I laughed at him and he laughed back, like a guilty small boy. He said, 'I really do, you know, it's not just a line. I really think you're the most attractive girl I've ever met.' Something like that. I didn't really listen to the words, because anyway I knew then in that tiny moment when we were laughing together so close that I had no hope. No hope at all.

TERENCE RATTIGAN (born 1911)
The Deep Blue Sea

False though she be to me and love,
  I'll ne'er pursue revenge;
For still the charmer I approve,
  Though I deplore her change.

In hours of bliss we oft have met:
  They could not always last;
And though the present I regret,
  I'm grateful for the past.

WILLIAM CONGREVE (1670–1729)
False Though She Be

'Dearest Maurice', she wrote, 'I meant to write to you the other night after you had gone away, but I felt rather sick when I got home and Henry fussed about me. I'm writing instead of telephoning. I can't telephone and hear your voice go queer when I say I'm not going to come away with you. Because I'm not going to come away with you, Maurice, dearest Maurice. I love you but I can't see you again. I don't know how I'm going to live in this pain and longing and I'm praying to God all the time that he won't be hard on me, that he won't keep me alive. Dear Maurice, I want to have my cake and eat it like everybody else. I went to a priest two days ago . . . and I told him I wanted to be Catholic. . . . I said, I'm not really married to Henry any more. We don't sleep together – not since the first year with you. . . . I asked him couldn't I be a Catholic and marry you? I knew you wouldn't mind going through a service. . . . No, no, no, he said, I couldn't marry you, I couldn't go on seeing you, not if I was going to be a Catholic. I thought, to hell with the whole lot of them and I walked out of the room where I was seeing him and I slammed the door to show what I thought of priests. They are between us and God, I thought; God has more mercy . . . only it's such an odd sort of mercy, it sometimes looks like punishment. Maurice, my dearest, I've got a foul headache, and I feel like death. I wish I weren't as strong as a horse. I don't want to live without you, and I know one day I shall meet you on the Common and then I won't care a damn about Henry or God or anything. But what's the good, Maurice? I believe there's a God. . . . I've caught belief like a disease. I've fallen into belief like I fell in love. I've never loved before as I love you, and I've never believed in anything before as I believe now. . . . I fought belief for longer than I fought love, but I haven't any fight left.

GRAHAM GREENE (born 1904)
The End of the Affair

MAID: Did you call, sir?

GENERAL: What? Who's that? No, I didn't call. Who are you?

MAID: I'm the new girl, sir. The new chambermaid you engaged this morning.

GENERAL: Oh yes, of course, by Jove, yes. And what is your name, my dear?

MAID: Pamela, sir.

GENERAL: Pamela. Fancy that now. Pamela. And the prettiest bosom in the world too. What is all this nonsense about a soul? Do you believe in it? . . . Put your broom down, my child. It's a bit late to be sweeping up now. And there is never enough dust on things. We must let it settle. You know, you'll find this an easy sort of place. I'm an old youngster and I don't ask for very much – provided folks are nice to me. You haven't seen my roses, have you? Come, I'll show you round the garden, and if you're a good girl I'll give you one – just like a real lady. It doesn't bother you, does it, Pamela, if I put my arm round your waist?

MAID: No sir, but what will Madam say?

GENERAL: Madam will say nothing so long as you don't tell her. That's a good girl. It's nicer like this, don't you think? Not that it means anything, but still, one feels less lonely, in the dark.

JEAN ANOUILH (born 1910)
The Waltz of the Toreadors

A thoroughly conventional man in good society would rather that his son should resort with prostitutes than that he should marry a respectable girl of a distinctly lower station than his own: indeed it is not going too far to say that he probably would rather his son should seduce such a girl, provided there were no scandal, than marry her.

THE REVD. HON. EDWARD LYTTELTON (1855–1942)
Headmaster of Eton

Here lie the bones of Elizabeth Charlotte
Born a virgin, died a harlot.
She was aye a virgin at seventeen
A remarkable thing in Aberdeen

An Aberdeen Epitaph

Sometimes a horrible marionette
Came out, and smoked its cigarette
Upon the steps like a live thing.

Then turning to my love, I said,
'The dead are dancing with the dead,
The dust is whirling with the dust.'

But she – she heard the violin,
And left my side, and entered in:
Love passed into the house of lust.

OSCAR WILDE (1854–1900)
The Harlot's House

[Jessica Mitford and her cousin have been left in Paris in the care of a 'reliable' Frenchwoman whom Lady Redesdale, Jessica's mother, fondly imagines is escorting the girls to the Opera in the evenings! Jessica's companion on this occasion is a middle-aged Frenchman; she is then about seventeen.]

After an hour or so at the *Bal Tabarin*, my companion suggested we should go somewhere else; he offered to show me 'le vrai Paris'. . . . We drove through the dark streets for some distance, finally arriving at what appeared to be an ordinary house in a row of dwellings. . . . A kindly-looking old French lady admitted us to a brightly-lit empty drawing-room. I felt all my new-found sophistication seeping out fast, and was hardly reassured when several naked girls appeared carrying champagne and glasses.

'This is one of the finest houses in Paris', my companion explained. 'Wouldn't you like to see the rest of it? . . .

We looked into a succession of rooms opening off a long corridor. Our guide explained that they were designed to cater to every imaginable preference. One was lined, floor to ceiling, with mirrors; another was full of statues and pictures of the Virgin Mary ('pour les pygmalionistes') she pointed out; yet another was a replica of a Pullman carriage, and our guide proudly showed how, by turning on a switch, the whole room could be made to shake and rumble like a real train, while artificial scenery appeared to move past the window. . . .

The room 'pour les sadistes' was the most amazing of all. . . . It was decorated like a torture-chamber, with racks, thumbscrews, whipping posts, realistic-looking plaster snails crawling over the rough stone walls. Two of the naked girls appeared and began to whip each other in a desultory sort of way. . . .

'I really do think it's about time we were getting along,' I said anxiously.

JESSICA MITFORD (born 1917)
Hons and Rebels

Liquor . . . gave him the courage to surmount his terrors and go to the brothel. . . . He drove to the door and resolutely rang the bell. Craftily he had chosen this forlorn, drizzly afternoon, hoping the red-plush salon would be empty, the girls idle.

'Come in, come in. Hurry up.' The rheumy-eyed slattern motioned him inside. . . .

She squinted at him not unkindly, as if sensing his apprehensiveness.

'You came at the right moment . . . there's nobody upstairs.'

A sudden suspicion came into her eyes. 'Even if you're a midget, you can make love, *hein*?' He nodded imperceptibly . . .

'Then everything's all right. Big and small, old and young – it's all the same to us. *L'amour*, that's what we're here for. Now you go upstairs and I'll call the girls.'

Grabbing the banister he hoisted himself up the steep, thin-carpeted stairs and pantingly hobbled into the dim, empty salon with its garnet *portières*, the worn plush banquettes behind the row of painted iron tables, the mechanical piano, the dusty palms in the corners, the fly-specked oleograph 'Cleopatra at the Bath' hanging between two gilt-framed mirrors, the smell of face powder and stale tobacco. The room had an air of tranquil abjection, the slimy peacefulness of a swamp. . . .

Above the hammering of his heart he heard footsteps, an indistinct babble of giggles and excited whispers in the hallway.

A hand parted the curtains. Five women's faces crowded into the opening and ten beady eyes focused upon him. . . . He watched a plump cow-eyed brunette cross the room towards him, her great breasts wobbling beneath her chemise.

'You don't know me, eh?' she beamed. 'But me, I know you. . . . I'm Berthe. . . . Your friend Rachou told me about you. . . .'

She turned to the girls who had cautiously followed her into the room, 'It's all right. He's an artist; he paints pictures. . . .'

The girls shook hands with him and with skittish little smiles took their places at table, blandly unaware of their nakedness. . . .

Octave, the waiter, turned on the gasolier and served a round of vermouth-cassis. Soon the first patrons began to arrive. Awkwardly they took their places on the red-plush banquettes, avoiding one another's eyes, twisting their caps in their hands.

One by one the girls rose and excused themselves. . . .

Henri watched them saunter over to the men, slip their arms around their necks, drone the ritual '*Alors, chéri*, you buy me a drink?' Someone started the mechanical piano. Night had come to *Le Perroquet Gris*.

Now only Berthe remained at his table.

'Perhaps you'd like to go upstairs?' she suggested remembering the object of his visit.

He nodded and followed her out of the room.

PIERRE LA MURE
Moulin Rouge
(Based on the life of Henri de Toulouse-Lautrec)

'Bonsoir, ma chérie,
Comment allez-vous ?'
'Je suis très bien,
Merci beaucoup.'
'Etes-vous fiancée ?'
'San fairy-ann.'
'Voulez-vous promenader avec moi ce soir ?'
'Oui, oui –
Combien ?'

Comrades in Arms: Conversation Piece

Men will pay large sums to whores
For telling them they are not bores.

W. H. Auden (1907–1973)

A nobleman, whom Cora Pearl in her memoirs disguises under the name Vicomte René Gontran de Cedar, gave her 76,000 francs (£3,040) in seven months – that is at the rate of some £5,000 a year. This generous protector also gave her 'a very comfortable landau' and other costly gifts. Cora notes, somewhat naïvely, that 'the Vicomte's family did not view our liaison with a benevolent eye.'

What did she get from Prince Napoleon? Exact figures are not available, but he provided her with a mansion of her own . . . a key to his grand apartments in the Palais Royal; servants, carriages, horses, furniture, plate and linen . . . and an allowance of 12,000 francs (£480) a month, of which, she says, she regularly spent £1,000!

It was at Baden-Baden, then the most fashionable spa-cum-gambling centre in the world, that Cora was gracefully sailing into the Kursaal, all dressed in white satin and white lace, on the arm of Salamanca . . . when they were very politely and firmly stopped by an official with a big gold chain round his neck, and Cora was told her presence would cause a scandal and she must retire. . . .

Within half an hour, Cora and her red hair and white

jewels and her interminable white dress again appeared in the doorway triumphant, for this time, being on the arm of the Duke of Hamilton . . . whose mother was a Princess of Baden, her progress was unimpeded; in fact, all the Casino officials bowed to the ground as she advanced.

MICHAEL HARRISON (born 1907)
Fanfare of Strumpets

Last night, ah, yesternight, betwixt her lips and mine
There fell thy shadow, Cynara! thy breath was shed
Upon my soul between the kisses and the wine;
And I was desolate and sick of an old passion,
  Yea, I was desolate and bow'd my head:
I have been faithful to thee, Cynara! in my fashion.

All night upon mine heart I felt her warm heart beat,
Night-long within mine arms in love and sleep she lay;
Surely the kisses of her bought red mouth were sweet;
But I was desolate and sick of an old passion,
  When I awoke and found the dawn was gray:
I have been faithful to thee, Cynara! in my fashion.

I have forgot much, Cynara! gone with the wind,
Flung roses, roses, riotously with the throng,
Dancing, to put thy pale lost lilies out of mind;
But I was desolate and sick of an old passion,
  Yea, all the time, because the dance was long:
I have been faithful to thee, Cynara! in my fashion.

I cried for madder music and for stronger wine,
But when the feast is finish'd and the lamps expire,
Then falls thy shadow, Cynara! the night is thine;
And I am desolate and sick of an old passion,
  Yea, hungry for the lips of my desire:
I have been faithful to thee, Cynara! in my fashion.

ERNEST DOWSON (1867–1900)
Non Sum Qualis Eram

Adulterers and customers of whores
And cunning takers of virginities
Caper from bed to bed, but not because
The flesh is pricked to infidelities.

The body is content with homely fare;
It is the avid, curious mind that craves
New pungent sauce and strips the larder bare,
The palate and not hunger that enslaves.

Don Juan never was a sensualist:
Scheming fresh triumphs, artful, wary, tense,
He took no pleasure in the breasts he kissed
But gorged his ravenous mind and starved each sense.

An itching, tainted intellectual pride
Guards the salt lecher till he has to know
Whether all women's eyes grow bright and wide,
All wives and whores and virgins shudder so.

Hunters of women burn to show their skill,
Yet when the panting quarry has been caught
Mere force of habit drives them to the kill:
The soft flesh is less savoury than their sport.

JOHN PRESS (born 1920)
Womanisers

George demanded worship, and was worshipped wherever he went. Women clustered round him, and he demanded from them the same absolute worship he received when he was playing the piano. Inevitably the women rebelled. They, too, wanted worship; they floated away and were replaced by others; a succession of mistresses danced fleetingly through his life.

He knew that something was wrong, and turned to psychiatrists for help. They were unable to help him, or fell under his spell. The parade of mistresses continued, underscoring his essential restlessness.

According to one of the psychiatrists who treated him, Gershwin's attitude to sex was comparable with that of a healthy and irresponsible adolescent. He enjoyed sexual encounters for their own sake and because they stimulated him to compose new musical themes. He was not unkind to his mistresses; it was simply that he felt he had a right to use them as part of his exploration of musical experience. He was a sexual athlete and sometimes slept with two women at once in his bed.

ROBERT PAYNE (born 1911)
Gershwin

It is as absurd to say that a man can't love one woman all the time as it is to say that a violinist needs several violins to play the same piece of music.

HONORÉ DE BALZAC (1799–1850)

Love, as it is practised in society, is merely the exchange of two momentary desires and the contact of two skins.

SÉBASTIEN CHAMFORT (1740/41–1794)

'Like men riding,
The mist from the sea
Drives down the valley
And baffles me.'
'Enter, traveller,
Whoever you be.'

By lamplight confronted
He staggered and peered;
Like a wet bramble
Was his beard.
'Sit down, stranger,
You look a-feared.'

Shudders rent him
To the bone,
The wet ran off him
And speckled the stone.
'Dost bide here alone, maid?'
'Yes, alone.'

As he sat down
In the chimney-nook
Over his shoulder
He cast a look,
As if the night
Were pursuing: she took

A handful of brash
To mend the fire,
As the flame shot higher;
He spoke– and the cattle
Moved in the byre.

'Though you should heap
Your fire with wood,
'Twouldn't warm me
Nor do no good
Unless you first warm me
As a maiden should.'

With looks unwavering,
With breath unstirred,
She took off her clothes
Without a word,
And stood up naked
And white as a curd.

He breathed her to him
With famished sighs,
Against her bosom
He sheltered his eyes,
And warmed his hand
Between her thighs.

Strangely assembled
In the quiet room,
Alone alight
Amidst leagues of gloom,
So brave a bride,
So sad a groom.

SYLVIA TOWNSEND WARNER (born 1893)
Nelly Trim

The feelings I don't have I don't have
The feelings I don't have, I won't say I have.
The feelings you say you have, you don't have.
The feelings you would like us both to have, we neither of
  us have.
The feelings people ought to have, they never have.
If people say they've got feelings, you may be pretty sure
  they haven't got them.
So if you want either of us to feel anything at all
You'd better abandon all idea of feelings altogether.

D. H. LAWRENCE (1885–1930)
To Women, As Far As I'm Concerned

How do you know love is gone? If you said that you would be there at seven, and you get there at nine, and he or she has not called the police yet – it's gone.

MARLENE DIETRICH (born 1904)

Why must you always think that love is for eternity? What do you mean when you say 'for life'? Our clothes change with the fashions; we move from one house to another; fruit goes rotten; flowers fade. . . . A doctor will tell you that after seven years there isn't a single cell in your body that hasn't changed. We change and decompose from the day we are born, and yet you still go on hoping that love will stay fresh and uncorrupted. Where did you learn to believe such things, you and your father? At school, or in trashy novels? Your heads are so full of second-hand romance that you've forgotten to learn how to live. If your father had started life as I did at thirteen in the *Folies Bergères*, he would have known better than to kill himself for love.

JEAN ANOUILH (born 1910)
Colombe
(translated by Denis Cannan)

[Edwin and Amy Reardon were very much in love, and at first enjoyed a happy marrige. It broke up because of desperate poverty. Edwin struggled to make a living as a writer, but was unsuccessful, and Amy left him because she could not stand the poverty any longer. Later she came into some money, and wrote to her estranged husband.]

Dear Edwin,

You must, of course, have heard . . . that my uncle John has left me ten thousand pounds. It has not yet come into my possession, and I had decided that I would not write to you till that happened, but perhaps you may altogether misunderstand my silence.

If this money had come to me when you were struggling so hard to earn a living for us, we should never have spoken the words and thought the thoughts which now make it so difficult for me to write to you. What I wish to say is that, although the property is legally my own, I quite recognize that you have a right to share in it. Since we have lived apart you have sent me far more than you could really afford, believing it your duty to do so; now that things are so different I wish you, as well as myself, to benefit by the change.

I said at our last meeting that I should be quite prepared to return to you if you took the position at Croydon. There is now no need for you to pursue a kind of work for which you are quite unfitted, and I repeat that I am willing to live with you as before. If you will tell me where you would like to make a new home I shall gladly agree. I do not think you would care to leave London permanently, and certainly I should not.

Please to let me hear from you as soon as possible. In writing like this I feel that I have done what you expressed a wish that I should do. I have asked you to put an end to our separation, and I trust that I have not asked in vain.

Yours always,
Amy Reardon

The letter fell from his hand. It was such a letter as he might have expected, but the beginning misled him, and as his agitation throbbed itself away he suffered an encroachment of despair which made him for a time unable to move or even think.

His reply, written by the dreary twilight which represented sunset, ran thus:

Dear Amy,

I thank you for your letter, and I appreciate your motive in writing it. But if you feel that you have 'done what I expressed a wish that you should do', you must have strangely misunderstood me.

The only thing that I *wished* was, that by some miracle your love for me might be revived. Can I persuade myself that this is the letter of a wife who desires to return to me because in her heart she loves me? If that is the truth you have been most unfortunate in trying to express yourself.

You have written because it seemed your duty to do so. But, indeed, a sense of duty such as this is a mistaken one. You have no love for me, and where there is no love there is no mutual obligation in marriage. Perhaps you think that regard for social conventions will necessitate your living with me again. But have more courage; refuse to act falsehoods; tell society it is base and brutal, and that you prefer to lead an honest life.

I cannot share your wealth, dear. But as you have no longer need of my help – as we are now quite independent of each other – I shall cease to send the money which hitherto I have considered yours. In this way I shall have enough, and more than enough, for my necessities, so that you will never have to trouble yourself with the thought that I am suffering privations. At Christmas I go to Croydon, and I will then write to you again.

For we may at all events be friendly. My mind is relieved from ceaseless anxiety on your account. I know now that you are safe from that accursed poverty which is to blame for all our sufferings. You I do not blame, though I have sometimes done so. My own experience teaches me how kindness can be embittered by misfortune. Some great and noble sorrow may have the effect of drawing hearts together, but to struggle againt destitution, to be crushed by care about shillings and sixpences – that must always degrade.

No other reply than this possible, so I beg you not to write in this way again....

Edwin Reardon

GEORGE GISSING (1857–1903)
New Grub Street

The band was playing a waltz-quadrille,
  I felt as light as wind-blown feather,
As we floated away, at the caller's will,
  Through the intricate, mazy dance together.
Like mimic armies our lines were meeting,
Slowly advancing, and then retreating,
  All decked in their bright array;
And back and forth to the music's rhyme
We moved together, and all the time
  I knew you were going away.

I said to my heart, 'Let us take our fill
  Of mirth, and music, and love, and laughter;
For it all must end with this waltz-quadrille,
  And life will be never the same life after.
Oh that the caller might go on calling!
Oh that the music might go on falling
  Like a shower of silver spray,
While we whirled on to the vast Forever,
Where no hearts break, and no ties sever,
  And no one goes away!'

A clamour, a crash, and the band was still,
 'Twas the end of the dream, and the end of the measure:
The last low notes of that waltz-quadrille
 Seemed like a dirge o'er the death of pleasure.
You said good-night, and the spell was over –
Too warm for a friend, and too cold for a lover –
 There was nothing else to say;
But the lights looked dim, and the dancers weary,
And the music was sad and the hall was dreary,
 After you went away.

ELLA WHEELER WILCOX (1850–1919)
A Waltz-Quadrille

The old story is true of charms fading;
He knew her first before her charm was mellow –
Slim; surprise in her eyes; like a woodland creature
Crept abroad who found the world amazing,

Who, afterwards maturing, yet was dainty,
Light on her feet and gentle with her fingers;
Put on a little flesh, became an easy
Spreadeagled beauty for Renaissance painters.

And then she went; he did not see her after
Until by the shore of a cold sea in winter
With years behind her and the waves behind her.
Drubbing the memory up and down the pebbles.

Flotsam and wrack; the bag of old emotions;
Watch in the swirl her ten years back reflections –
White as a drowning hand, then gone for ever;
Here she stands who was twenty and is thirty.
The same but different and he found the difference
A surgeon's knife without an anaesthetic;
He had known of course that this happens
But had not guessed the pain of it or the panic,

And could not say 'My love', could hardly
Say anything at all, no longer knowing
Whom he was talking to but watched the water
Massing for action on the cold horizon.

LOUIS MACNEICE (1907–1963)
The Old Story

Tuesday s'ennight a man named John Osborne, who lived at Godhurst, came to Maidstone for the purpose of disposing of his wife by sale; but it not being market day the auction was removed to the sign of the Coal Barge in Earl Street where she was actually sold to a man named William Sergeant, with her child, for the sum of £1. The business was conducted in a very regular manner, a deed and covenant being given by the seller, of which the following is a literal copy: 'I, John Osborne, doth agree to part with my wife, Mary Osborne, and child, to William Serjeant, for the sum of one pound, in consideration of giving up all claim whatever, whereunto I have made my mark as an acknowledgement. Maidstone, Jan. 3rd 1815.'

JOHN ASHTON (1880–1952)
Social Life in the Reign of Queen Anne

What God hath joined together no man shall ever put asunder: God will take care of that.

GEORGE BERNARD SHAW (1856–1950)

The train at Pershore station was waiting that Sunday night
Gas light on the platform, in my carriage electric light,
Gas light on frosty evergreens, electric on Empire wood,
The Victorian world and the present in a moment's neighbourhood.
There was no one about but a conscript who was saying good-bye to his love
On the windy weedy platform with the sprinkled stars above
When sudden the waiting stillness shook with the ancient spells
Of an older world than all our worlds in the sound of the Pershore bells.
They were ringing them down for Evensong in the lighted abbey near,
Sounds which had poured through apple boughs for seven centuries here.
With Guilt, Remorse, Eternity the void within me fills
And I thought of her left behind me in the Herefordshire hills.
I remembered her defencelessness as I made my heart a stone
Till she wove her self-protection round and left me on my own.
And plunged in a deep self pity I dreamed of another wife
And lusted for freckled faces and lived a separate life.
One word would have made her love me, one word would have made her turn
But the word I never murmured and now I am left to burn.
Evesham, Oxford and London. The carriage is new and smart.
I am cushioned and soft and heated with a deadweight in my heart.

JOHN BETJEMAN (born 1906)
Pershore Station, or *A Liverish Journey First Class*

Winter

This night late, coming in my coach . . . up Ludgate Hill, I saw two gallants and their footmen taking a pretty wench which I have much eyed lately, set up shop upon the hill, a seller of ribband and gloves. They seemed to drag her by some force, but the wench went and I believe had her turn served; but God forgive me, what thoughts and wishes I had of being in their place.

SAMUEL PEPYS (1633–1703)
Diary
February 1664

Love-philtre, Love potion. A potion, drug or charm supposedly having the power to excite sexual passion, especially towards a particular person.

Webster's Third New International Dictionary

If a man mixes the powder of the milk hedge plant and the kantaka plant with the excrement of a monkey and the powdered root of the lanjalika plant, and throws this mixture on a woman, she will not love anybody else afterwards.

The Kama Sutra of Vatsayana

Of all aphrodisiacs the best known and the most used is probably food. Professor McCary points out that there is a closer and deeper connection between eating and sexual desire than is generally realized. . . . 'When', he says, 'one has eaten a carefully prepared, subtly seasoned meal, together with wine, in an "ambiance" enhanced by soft music and glowing candles, one experiences a delightful glow – not only of the senses, but also of the body – a feeling that can hardly be present after one has consumed a . . . meal of meat loaf, boiled potatoes, and watery beans in a boarding house. . . .'

PHILIPPA PULLAR (born 1935)
Consuming Passions

[*Lines written upon hearing the startling news that cocoa is, in fact, a mild aphrodisiac*]

Half-past nine – high time for supper;
'Cocoa, love?' 'Of course, my dear.'
Helen thinks it quite delicious,
John prefers it now to beer.
Knocking back the sepia potion,
Hubby winks, says 'Who's for bed?'
'Shan't be long', says Helen softly,
Cheeks a faintly flushing red.
For they've stumbled on the secret
Of a love that never wanes,
Rapt beneath the tumbled bedclothes,
Cocoa coursing through their veins.

STANLEY J. SHARPLESS
In Praise of Cocoa, Cupid's Nightcap

Nothing dies so quickly in the heart of the woman as the love that has been orchestrated by the man upon the strings of the tear ducts. Nothing lives on so fresh and ever green as the love with a funny-bone.

GEORGE JEAN NATHAN (1882–1958)
The Enduring Love

Among those whom I like or admire, I can find no common denominator, but among those whom I love, I can: all of them make me laugh.

W. H. AUDEN (1907–1973)
Notes on the Comic

Hygienist, in your dental chair
I sit without a single care,
Except when tickled by your hair.
I know that when you grab the drills
I need not fear the pain that kills.
You merely make my molars clean
With pumice doped with wintergreen.
So I lean back with calm reflection,
With close-up views of your complexion,
And taste the flavor of your thumbs
While you massage my flabby gums.
To me no woman can be smarter
Than she who scales away my tartar,
And none more fitted for my bride
Than one who knows me from inside.
At least as far as she has gotten
She sees how much of me is rotten.

EARNEST A. HOOTON (1887–1954)
Ode to a Dental Hygienist

Flirting. An accomplishment which is at twenty a joy, at thirty a pastime, at forty a habit, and at fifty a pose.

Wanting for their young limbs praise,
Their thighs, hips, and saintly breasts,
They grow from awkwardness to delight,
Their mouths made perfect with the air
About them and the sweet rage in the blood,
The delicate trouble in their veins.

Intolerant as happiness, suddenly
They'll dart like bewildered birds;
For there's no mercy in that bugler Time
That excites against their virginity
The massed infantry of days, nor in the tendrils
Greening on their enchanted battlements.

Golda, Fruma, Dinnie, Elinor,
My saintly wantons, passionate nuns;
O light-footed daughters, your unopened
Brittle beauty troubles an aging man
Who hobbles after you a little way
Fierce and ridiculous.

IRVING LAYTON (born 1912)
To the Girls of My Graduating Class

At the age of sixty, to marry a beautiful girl of sixteen is to imitate those ignorant people who buy books to be read by their friends.

LOUIS XAVIER RICARD (1843–1911)

Don't ever marry an old man
I'll tell you the reason why
His lips are all tobacco juice
And his chin is never dry.

For an old man he is old
And an old man he is grey
But a young man's heart is full of love
Get away, old man, get away.

Victorian Ballad

A small religious community in Applegate, California, has lost all but the two founder members, Mr William Corecco, aged 89, and his brother Stephen, aged 91, after they insisted upon 'absolute abstinence from sexual activity as a prerequisite for membership'.

Said Mr William, 'We expected a heavy fall-out, but nothing like this.'

Yorkshire Evening Post
17 June 1971

Love and eggs are best when they are fresh.

A gentleman who had been very unhappy in marriage married immediately after his wife died. Dr Johnson said, it was the triumph of hope over experience.

JAMES BOSWELL (1740–1795)
Life of Johnson

When Queen Caroline, the consort of King George II, lay dying, she urged her husband to marry again. He replied tenderly: 'No, I shall have mistresses.'

He [Tiberius] no longer made any serious attempt to conceal his sexual depravity, the rumours of which everyone had shrunk from taking literally. For some of his perversities were so preposterous and horrible that nobody could seriously reconcile them with the dignity of an Emperor of Rome. . . . No women or boys were safe in his presence now, even the wives and children of senators; and if they valued their own lives or those of their husbands and fathers they willingly did what he expected of them. But one woman, a consul's wife, committed suicide afterwards in the presence of her friends, telling them that she had been forced to save her young daughter from Tiberius's lust by consenting to prostitute herself to him which was shameful enough; but then the old He-Goat had taken advantage of her complaisance by forcing her to such abominable acts of filthiness with him that she preferred to die than to live on with the memory of them.

ROBERT GRAVES (born 1895)
I, Claudius

Daudet's thoughts ran on a single theme. Dining with Zola one night he was given grouse. He compared it 'to an old courtesan's flesh marinaded in a bidet'.

EDMOND (1822–1896) and JULES (1830–1870)
DE GONCOURT
Journal

And next to him rode lustful Lechery,
Upon a bearded Goat, whose rugged haire,
And Whally eyes (the signs of gelosy),
Was like the person selfe, whom he did beare,
Who rough, and blacke, and filthy did appeare,
Unseemly man to please fair Ladies' eye;
Yet he of Ladies oft was loved deare,
When fairer faces were bid standen by:
O who does know the bent of women's fantasy?

EDMUND SPENSER (?1552–1599)
The Faerie Queene (Lust)

I'll come no more behind your scenes, David [Garrick]; for the silk stockings and white bosoms of your actresses excite my amorous propensities.

JAMES BOSWELL (1740–1795)
Life of Johnson

Why blush, dear girl, pray tell me why?
  You need not, I can prove it;
For though your garter met my eye,
  My thoughts were far above it.

Pretty round heaving breast, a Barbary shape, and a jut with her bum would stir an anchorite, and the prettiest foot! Oh, if a man could but fasten his eyes to her feet as they steal in and out and play at bo-peep under her petticoats!

William Congreve (1670–1729)
Love for Love

Be quiet, Sir! Begone, I say!
Lord bless us! How you romp and tear!
There!
I swear!
Now you left my bosom bare!
I do not like such boisterous play,
So take that saucy hand away –
Why now, you're ruder than before!
Nay, I'll be hanged if I comply –
Fie!
I'll cry!
Oh – I can't bear it – I shall die!
I vow I'll never see you more!
But – are you sure you've shut the door?

Is this London? Is this the year 1872? . . . Weary of surveying the poetry of the past, and listening to the amatory wails of generations, I walk down the streets, and lo! again harlots stare from the shopwindows. . . . I walk in the broad day, and a dozen hands offer me indecent prints. . . . I buy a cheap republican newspaper, thinking that there, at least, I shall find some relief, if only in the wildest stump oratory, and I am saluted instead in these words: '*Fanny Hill*. Genuine edition, illustrated. Two volumes, 2s. 6d. each. . . .'

Stop where I may, the snake Sensualism spits its venom upon me. . . . Photographs of nude, indecent, and hideous harlots, in every possible attitude that vice can devise, flaunt from the shop-windows, gloated over by the fatuous glint of the libertine and the greedy open-mouthed stare of the day-labourer. Never was this snake . . . so vital and poisonous as now. It has penetrated into the very sweetshops; and there, among the commoner sorts of confectionary, may be seen this year models of the female leg, the whole definite and elegant article as far as the thighs, with a fringe of paper cut in imitation of the female drawers and embroidered in the female fashion!

ROBERT BUCHANAN (1841–1901)
The Fleshly School Of Poetry

Fortunes Are Being Made From The Trade In Dirty Books
Informed guesses, on the conservative side, suggested that so-called 'hard pornography' represents at least £10 million-a-year turnover and 'soft pornography' many times that amount.

Hard-core books and magazines sell for £6 and £7. 'Private', described as 'an internationally notorious erotic magazine', printed in four languages costs £5 an issue in Britain.

The most objectionable marketing is that carried on through the post, and accounts for the greater part of the trade in hard pornography.

As in other areas where risks and profits were high, there was a danger of gang warfare, protection rackets and intimidation. There is some evidence of these, notably in London.

The Longford Report
The Daily Telegraph
20 September 1972

My head is bald, my breath is bad,
  Unshaven is my chin,
I have not now the joys I had
  When I was young in sin.

I run my fingers down your dress
  With brandy-certain aim
And you respond to my caress
  And maybe feel the same.

But I've a picture of my own
  On this reunion night,
Wherein two skeletons are shewn
  To hold each other tight;

Dark sockets look on emptiness
  Which once was loving-eyed,
The mouth that opens for a kiss
  Has got no tongue inside.

I cling to you inflamed with fear
  As now you cling to me,
I feel how frail you are my dear
  And wonder what will be –

A week ? or twenty years remain ?
  And then – what kind of death ?
A losing fight with frightful pain
  Or a gasping fight for breath ?

Too long we let our bodies cling,
  We cannot hide disgust
At all the thoughts that in us spring
  From this late flowering lust.

JOHN BETJEMAN (born 1906)
Late Flowering Lust

Thou blind-man's mark, thou fool's self-chosen snare,
Fond fancy's scum, and dregs of scattered thought;
Band of all evils, cradle of causeless care;
Thou web of will, whose end is never wrought;
Desire, desire! I have too dearly bought,
With price of mangled mind, thy worthless ware;
Too long, too long, asleep thou hast me brought,
Who should my mind to higher things prepare.
But yet in vain thou hast my ruin sought;
In vain thou madest me to vain things aspire;
In vain thou kindlest all thy smoky fire;
For virtue hath this better lesson taught,
Within myself to seek my only hire,
Desiring nought but how to kill desire.

PHILIP SIDNEY (1554–1586)
Thou Blind-Man's Mark

Now heaven be thanked, I am out of love again!
I have been long a slave, and now am free;
I have been tortured, and am eased of pain;
I have been blind, and now my eyes can see;
I have been lost, and now my way lies plain;
I have been caged, and now I hold the key;
I have been mad, and now at last am sane;
I am wholly I that was but half of me.
So a free man, my dull proud path I plod,
Who, tortured, blind, mad, caged, was once a God.

JAN STRUTHER (1901–1953)
Freedom

She parried time's malicious dart,
And kept the years at bay,
Till passion entered in her heart
And aged her in a day!

ELLA WHEELER WILCOX (1850–1919)

When you are old and grey and full of sleep
And nodding by the fire, take down this book,
And slowly read, and dream of the soft look
Your eyes had once, and of their shadows deep;

How many loved your moments of glad grace,
And loved your beauty with love false or true;
But one man loved the pilgrim soul in you,
And loved the sorrows of your changing face;

And bending down beside the glowing bars,
Murmur, a little sadly, how love fled
And paced upon the mountains overhead,
And hid his face amid a crowd of stars.

W. B. YEATS (1865–1939).
When You Are Old

Remember me when I am gone away,
  Gone far away into the silent land;
  When you can no more hold me by the hand,
Nor I half turn to go, yet turning stay.
Remember me when no more day by day
  You tell me of our future that you plann'd;
  Only remember me; you understand
It will be late to counsel then or pray.
Yet if you should forget me for a while
  And afterwards remember, do not grieve:
  For if the darkness and corruption leave
  A vestige of the thoughts that once I had,
Better by far you should forget and smile
  Than that you should remember and be sad.

CHRISTINA ROSSETTI (1830–1894)
Remember

I ended the last volume of my father's Diaries with Vita's funeral. During his lifetime I did not wish to dwell on his agony. 'Oh Vita, I have wept buckets for you', he wrote three weeks later. And he did, quietly at the dinner-table, clamourously when he thought himself out of ear-shot in the garden. I was awed by his desolation, giving him the comfort of my familiar presence, but fearing to increase his flow of tears by attempting to staunch them by words of consolation or remembrance. He never recovered from Vita's death. His gaiety gradually subsided into gentle good humour, his intellectual vitality to vague contemplation. He had two strokes in quick succession, which further dulled his mind. . . . Sometimes I would ask him about the past, but his responses became fewer. He told me that he had no wish to live longer, and I believed him.

The end was sudden and merciful. He died at Sissinghurst on 1 May 1968, of a heart attack, as he was undressing for bed.

NIGEL NICOLSON (born 1917)
Portrait of a Marriage

If I should learn, in some quite casual way,
That you were gone, not to return again –
Read from the back-page of a paper, say,
Held by a neighbour in a subway train,
How at the corner of this avenue
And such a street (so are the papers filled)
A hurrying man – who happened to be you –
At noon today had happened to be killed,
I should not cry aloud – I could not cry
Aloud, or wring my hands in such a place –
I should but watch the station lights rush by
With a more careful interest in my face,
Or raise my eyes and read with greater care
Where to store furs and how to treat the hair.

EDNA ST VINCENT MILLAY (1892–1950)
Unnamed Sonnet

My dead Love came to me, and said:
'God gives me one hour's rest
To spend upon the earth with thee:
How shall we spend it best?'

'Why, as of old', I said, and so
We quarrell'd as of old.
But when I turn'd to make my peace
That one short hour was told.

STEPHEN PHILLIPS (1864–1916)
The Apparition

Call it a good marriage –
For no one ever questioned
Her warmth, his masculinity,
Their interlocking views;
Except one stray graphologist
Who frowned in speculation
At her h's and her s's,
His p's and w's.

Though few would still subscribe
To the monogamic axiom
That strife below the hip-bones
Need not estrange the heart,
Call it a good marriage:
More drew these two together,
Despite a lack of children,
Than pulled them apart.

Call it a good marriage.
They never fought in public,
They acted circumspectly
And faced the world with pride;
Thus the hazards of their love-bed
Were none of our damned business –
Till as juryman we sat on
Two deaths by suicide.

ROBERT GRAVES (born 1895)
Call It a Good Marriage

This handsome pair,
All mortal sharing done,
Rest in each other's arms,
Bound by a common shroud.

The gossamer gravecloth
Sculptured in supple bas-relief,
Purls like a shallow stream around
The stone-fixed sleepers.

Not like the chapelled pairs
That keep their decorous sleep
In rigid parallel, hands pointing
Heavenward, renouncing touch.

The woman holds her lover close
As though to bend his head down
For her kiss. His arm
Guards her. In the stone box

Bones and dust mingle.
The lovers who pause here,
Hands tight-locked, hearts chilled
At the thought of final sundering,
Envy these effigies.

RUTH FELDMAN
Sarcophagus Cover

LOUIS.

Index